Praise for
SMILER'S BONES
by Peter Lerangis

"*Smiler's Bones* is profoundly moving."
— Gary Paulsen, Newbery Award–winning author of *Hatchet*

"Lerangis offers a hugely fascinating novel, closely based on a true story. The writing is vivid, the description of New York City by a boy who had never even seen a tree before is particularly brilliant. . . . A compelling and important story."
— *Kirkus Reviews*

"Peter Lerangis's *Smiler's Bones* is a great read. Lerangis transcends the usual limits of 'young adult' and 'historical' fiction to give us a hybrid that's deeply moving and unforgettable."
— Terry Trueman, Printz Honor author of *Stuck in Neutral*

"In this wrenching first novel, based on true events, Lerangis gives voice to Minik, an Eskimo boy who, along with his father and several other villagers, was delivered to New York by Arctic explorer Robert Peary 'in the interest of science.'. . . The incisive emotions are unforgettable — all the more because they are culled from historical fact."
— *Booklist*

"A wonderful historical fiction adventure tale . . . this compelling story will keep readers interested until the last page."
— *VOYA*

SMILER'S BONES

PETER LERANGIS

SMILER'S BONES

SCHOLASTIC INC.

New York Toronto London Auckland Sydney
Mexico City New Delhi Hong Kong Buenos Aires

No part of this publication may be reproduced, stored in a retrieval system, or transmitted in any form or by any means, electronic, mechanical, photocopying, recording, or otherwise, without written permission of the publisher. For information regarding permission, write to Scholastic Inc., Attention: Permissions Department, 557 Broadway, New York, NY 10012.

ISBN-13: 978-0-439-34488-3

ISBN-10: 0-439-34488-3

12 11 10 9 8 7 6 5 4 3 2 1   7 8 9 10 11 12/0

Printed in the U.S.A.   40

First Scholastic paperback printing, February 2007

For Tina

Contents

Part Three: Quebec, May 7, 1909

Part One
Quebec, May 7, 1909

May 7, 1909

"Go right!" the priest says. "*À droite!*"

The carriage driver heads down an alleyway that slopes toward the water. I lie in the backseat, drenched in my own sweat, struggling to awaken.

This is how it has been since the pneumonia returned, sleep and waking, light and dark, summer and winter battling for my soul. I slip into a dream, and in it I am dry and happy on a sled, gliding home across the ice with my father. As the dogs veer to the left, he shouts to them, his voice sharp and clear in the bitter wind: *Attuk . . .*

"*Attuk . . . attuuuk . . .*" I mutter.

But instead of going right, the dogs leap off the ice and fly toward the sun. My father is laughing as usual, his face blessed with happiness and smiles in opposite measure to my own face's seriousness, as if I had been born to protect him instead of the other way around. Warily I lean over the sled runners and look down to try to signal to my mother. The clouds below us are white and thick like snow. When they break, I can see our village on Smith Sound, but it has changed. Instead of rock and ice and peat huts, I see cobblestone roads and stone towers, telegraph wires and smoke-spewing furnaces. And I hear a voice: *Kiiha Takeqihunga!*

The words that changed my life.

I sit bolt upright in the seat. "*Naan!*"

"I beg your pardon?" the priest asks. He is trim and graying, his blue eyes radiating a patience borne of listening to countless inner secrets.

"Nothing," I say. "A dream."

He hands me a handkerchief. As I mop my brow, he turns toward the carriage driver. Pointing to the last house on the alley, he says, "*Ici. Ah, bon.*"

We stop at a boardinghouse, a *pension*, four stories high. Its brick is mottled by peeling white paint. Next door is a small café overlooking the Rue Dalhousie, which follows the curve of the Saint Lawrence River along the southern edge of Quebec City.

The priest hops out of the carriage. Leaning in, he extends his arm for me. "May I?"

He knows something is wrong.

"I am fine," I say, although every part of me aches. Despite the fact that I'm nineteen years old, I feel ancient.

I climb out of the carriage, taking my own suitcase. It isn't much, a small, battered valise I found discarded on the street in Montreal. Affixed to the side is an Olympic Games symbol, also found in the trash. I keep that side turned out, visible as I walk to the boardinghouse. Inside it is everything I own, including my most valuable possession, a photograph of my father and me.

"I reserved you the room on the top floor, overlooking the river," the priest says. "It has a balcony."

I squint, looking up into the sunlight. The balcony is good. It will fit my plan just right.

The priest makes the financial arrangements at the front desk and takes the room key. I thank him and assure him that I will repay the fee.

"You will have to pay my friend and yours, Mr. Green, in Montreal," the priest says with a smile. "He sent me the money and asked me to be sure you rest up for your footrace. You are a very lucky young man that he knows someone in Quebec City."

"I am grateful." I hold out my hand for the key. "I will be fine now. I must sleep."

"Shall I have the front desk contact the Olympic Committee for you?"

"No, thank you."

"They'll be eager to know you have arrived."

"I will tell them."

"Splendid." The priest hesitates, then gives me the key. "May I join you for dinner later, Qivitoq?"

The name startles me for a moment. Illness has dulled my memory, and memory is necessary to sustain lies. I consider telling him the truth, that my name is not Qivitoq, that I will not be available for dinner, that I intend to be with my father. Instead I merely agree.

I wait for him to leave and then begin climbing the stairs. A momentary fit of coughing stops me at the first landing. When I reach the door, I must hold the jamb to stay upright.

The room is tiny. The bed's white wrought-iron frame is chipped and rusted, its horsehair mattress sunken in the middle as if someone invisible were still sleeping there. On one side is a night table with a drawer, on the other a wardrobe open to reveal three wooden hangers and a brass chamber pot. By the balcony window is a bureau, scarred by burnt cigarettes and supporting a gas lamp and a mirrorless oval frame into which someone has pasted a drawing of the Château Frontenac.

It is lonely, but it doesn't lack a shabby sort of dignity. A fitting place for me, I suppose.

I turn to the window. My task is easy. I could accomplish it right now, and perhaps I should. The priest will certainly return.

How will he understand what I am about to do? How could he ever link together the chain of events that led me here? He and Mr. Green have been kind to me. I owe them a letter of explanation, like the one I have already sent to Dob.

None of them will understand. Certainly not Dob. I suppose I should have been formal with his letter and addressed it to Roswell Chester Beecroft. But I have always called him "Dob" — Dear Old Beecroft — and he won't expect any different. Of all my friends, he has been truest.

This will not take much time. I sit on the bed and search the night table drawer for supplies. I find a pencil and an old leather-bound Bible, from which I tear an onionskin that is protecting a color reproduction of Jesus on the Mount.

But as I settle back to write, my eyelids grow heavy. The mattress, scratchy and stiff, feels to me like a pile of goose down.

I find myself drifting into another world, a place I'd left behind moments ago in the carriage.

The beginning.

Once again, I hear the words, loud and clear.

Piuli, 1893

"Kiiha Takeqihunga!"

It always begins this way — "I have come!" — shouted across the sea as he approaches. But at age three, maybe four, I don't know that yet.

I am at the top of the hill, above the bay, playing with my doll, Qunualuq. He has been sewn from sealskin by my mother, and his name means *one who smiles*. He reminds me of my father. He also reminds me, a bit, of me. I pretend he is subduing a fierce polar bear.

That is when I hear the far-off cry. And I see the beast.

It comes on the wind, and yet no wind could be powerful enough to move it. Wings rise from its back, fanning upward and outward, stealing the sunlight — enormous hides stretched over enormous bones, fretted with sinew like the traces of a dogsled. In our cove I have seen icebergs this size which, with a languid roll to one side, will capsize every kayak, every *umiaq*, in the harbor. But nothing compares to this. With a thunderous *foom . . . FOOM!* it plows into the ice floes, and its shadow slowly passes over me.

Innerajuaitsiat, I think. A giant spirit.

Then it begins to drop babies into the water.

"*Anaana!*" I scream, running down the hill toward my mother, Mannik. Along with another woman, Aleqasina, she is watching the men take kayaks into the bay.

From behind I hear footsteps crunching on the rocks. My father's arms surround me and lift me off the ground.

"No — it will eat us all!" I cry, kicking to get loose.

"What will?" my father asks.

"*Innerajuaitsiat!* In the water!"

He nuzzles his nose into the crook of my neck, and the tickle of his sparse black whiskers makes me giggle despite myself. "The *qallunaaqs* have come," he says. "That's all."

I feel myself rising onto my father's shoulders. I clutch Qunualuq to my face. As we come closer to the shore, I begin to see the distant floating objects in the bay more clearly.

The "babies" are boats, long ones like our *umiaqs*. Aboard them, pulling oars, are odd-looking men. Many wear hats. Their faces are hairy and their coats cling close to their bodies, as if the fur lining has been ripped out and applied directly to their chins. My father has told me that I have met some of these men, but I was little and I don't recall. I do, however, remember stories of them. They are white giants. They use fire to burn meat before they eat it. They blow smoke from little white shards they put in their mouths. They have metal and know-how to make knives, guns, and needles. They hunt with no rules or respect for the dead — without even pouring fresh water into the mouth of a killed seal. They don't sing. They build igloos only with wood. Their leader's name is Piuli.

As these men approach I examine their faces, pink and

9

brown and cragged. One of them is darker than we are. I conclude that my father is mistaken. These aren't *qallunaaqs* at all. "They are not white," I announce.

My father is bouncing me up and down now, lifting my right hand to wave to the approaching ship. He sings in a reedy voice to a made-up tune:

"Aya-ya-ya, aya-ya-ya,
Spirit of the sea,
Come forth with your wings and take us away,
To the place where light and dark come every day:
Where no one starves and no one suffers,
And no one is happy.
Open your belly and swallow us,
But promise to spit us back someday —
Aya-ya-ya . . . !"

He pulls me down and pretends to eat me. All around us, other children are racing to the shore. Two hundred thirty people live in our village — the only people I have ever seen — and they are all here. Shouting, waving, laughing. Some are calling "Piuli!" and "Piulerriaq!"

The first vessel lands, and out steps the largest man I have ever seen. His body seems to unfold in sections, and at full height he's the size of two or three of me. His beard is so thick and red I assume it is made of seaweed. As the children swarm around him, his upper lip lifts slightly to reveal a line of clenched teeth. He barks a laugh — a solid, well-formed "Haw!" — followed by an audible snapping shut of

10

his jaw. Then he hauls a barrel out of the boat, crying, *"Kiiha Takeqihunga!"* again in a dry, oddly high-pitched voice that disappears like a bird's in the wind. When he turns the barrel over, a thousand biscuits clatter onto the rocks.

At first I think the small, brittle objects are bones. What else could they be? But the children dive into the pile, giddy with laughter. They eat greedily, crazily, and white mush forms on their mouths.

I am scared out of my wits.

"Smiler!" calls the tall, bearded man. Even now I remember the sound of the two syllables — but it is not my father's name. He is Qisuk.

My father grins and takes my hand. "Come," he says, "meet Piulerriaq!"

I pull back.

"SMILER!" comes the call again, louder.

My father runs to the great Piuli, who points him toward a boat full of bulging canvas bags. Some of the men have already started carrying bags to Piuli's hut, a frame building down the coast. As my father joins them, Piuli turns to face me. His eyes are the color of ice.

At that moment I hear a deep, muted scream from the shore. Another boat has landed, and on it is a ghastly brown creature, snorting and bucking on four thin legs. Some of the children have gathered to see it.

Something strikes me sharply on the forehead, and I cry out.

Piuli has thrown me a biscuit. It bounces among the rocks and breaks into pieces.

11

Uisaakassak, a young man who is more like an overgrown boy, laughs at my clumsiness. One by one, the other children join him in laughter. The noise rings out over the rocky shore, until even the grown-ups and *qallunaaqs* join in.

I am afraid that Piuli will be angry at me. But he is distracted by Aleqasina, who puts her arms around him and touches his nose with a kiss. Aleqasina's husband stands by, grinning proudly.

I reach down and examine one of the biscuit pieces. Not trusting it, I put it to my doll Qunualuq's mouth first. He seems to think it is fine, so I try it myself.

The sweetness is a shock. It gives me a sense of pleasure like *mattak,* raw seal meat, but it is sharper and more immediate. I want more.

I race to the shore. Piuli is walking away with Aleqasina toward the hut, to the encouragement of some of his mates. But the dark man is smiling at me, reaching among the greedy children to hold out a handful of biscuits.

"*Mamakto,*" he says.

Tasty.

The Borders of a World

The dark man's face is fading.

The years disperse in a blizzard of fragmentary images, and then I am six years old. Around me the walls are ice blocks and frozen peat, the roof fortified by whalebone. The floor is a rubble of stones and I am looking down at a figure on a sealskin pallet who is glistening with sweat, forehead matted with black hair.

I hold tightly to Qunualuq. He is now brown and ragged, seasoned by years of saliva and snow, frozen and thawed and often repaired. I'm in the igloo of my father's friend Nuktaq. The figure is my mother.

The dark-skinned man speaks to me again, comforting words in Eskimo language. He is the only one of the *qallu-naaqs* who has learned to do this.

We call him Mahri-Pahluk. It means Matthew the Kind One. He is Matthew Henson and he takes orders from the man we know as Piuli — Robert Peary. This amuses my father, the idea of one man making decisions for others. We do not operate this way. Our men and women hunt, sew, flense, build, sing, dance, tell stories, each to the extent of his or her skill. Nonetheless, we do Peary's bidding, because he has

13

become our friend, because he gives us things we need, and because pleasing our guests is simply our way.

It has been three years since the first time I saw the *qallunaaqs*. I am no longer scared of them, or of biscuits.

I am, however, scared of death.

My mother is very, very ill. She has been sneezing, coughing. I kneel and take her hand, which has grown cold. "Qunualuq will take care of you," I say.

"Yes, I will!" I say in Qunualuq's voice, which sounds very much like my father.

My mother does not respond. Behind me Nuktaq's wife, Atangana, lets out a moan. She is a powerful shaman and has been calling on the *toorngat*, the helping spirits. Her work is exhausting, and she has collapsed against the wall. I stare at my mother, expecting her to rise, waiting for the spirits to enter her body.

"Please, little one," my father whispers thickly, "the burial must begin right away. We cannot allow her spirit to wander in anger."

He takes me gently in his arms, but I cannot feel him at all. I cannot feel anything.

As I back away, I realize that others have entered the igloo. Peary stands erect, his brow furrowed as if examining a chart. I have grown used to seeing him with Aleqasina, but he has avoided her since the arrival of Mrs. Peary. She stands beside him now, looking grim and uncomfortable as she always does. The Pearys' little daughter, Marie, who likes to think she can speak "Eskimo," says, "Ak . . . ok . . . took . . . meek," until Mrs. Peary quietly scolds her.

14

Peary announces something to Mahri-Pahluk, who translates: "Mannik was the best seamstress in the colony."

"*Qajanaq*," says my father. Thank you.

But I think of a day last Arctic winter when I wandered sightless and lost, the blowing snow black as the sky. To walk would have been futile; to yell would have meant choking on snow. So I stood, awaiting the spirit of Death, and soon saw a figure bright as fire in the darkness, hovering closer. "Come," the glowing vision said, taking my arm. It was not Death but my mother, who gently led me home.

I remember a storm that piled snow against our walls too thick to dig through. We took shallow breaths, fearful of using up the air and being buried alive. But the Eskimo word for breath, *anerca*, also means *poetry*, and as my mother prepared our seal meat, she began to sing. Soon the storm quieted its shrieking to listen. She lowered her sweet voice until the wind, no longer able to hear, blew away the muffling wall of snow and the sun streamed through the opening. And we ate.

A seamstress, yes. But more. She was sunlight and music, food and warmth, strength and love.

I bury my face in my father's coat and breathe deeply, taking what comfort I can from the familiar sweetly bitter mix of bearskin, smoke, and dried blood. It is a different smell from my mother's. I realize that in the dark this is how I know my parents. It is by their smells that I know the borders of my world.

Soon my father rises and the ceremony begins. He speaks to my mother's body in a stern voice, daring her to waken. Then he commands her spirit to visit only in dreams, never while he is awake. He and Nuktaq lay her body on a bearskin, place a mask over her face, then lay another skin over her. They carry her outside, placing her on the ground. Making sure her head is pointed away from the sea, they cover her body with stones. My father makes a mark in the ground, between her and our house.

I have seen the ritual. Others have died recently, from the same sickness. I know that over the next ten days my father will stay indoors, always wearing a hat, with a cord tied around his waist. In the mornings he will make a mark on the ground with a bone fragment, then take a walk around the igloo. Each morning the circle will grow wider until, on the tenth day, he will visit the grave.

Atangana has revived, and now she is wailing, over and over, "*Tornarsuk!*" Evil spirit!

"She is crazy," Uisaakassak whispers to me, brushing away tears. "Seven others have died, also. Healthy people who have worked hard and never been sick all their lives. *Tornarsuk* has never caused sickness like this."

When I look at him, baffled and confused, he scowls at me.

"It only happens," he says, "when the *qallunaaqs* are here."

Qivitoq

I am awakened by the door's creak. The priest peeks in. He is carrying a small package. "Perhaps I should come back later."

"I overslept," I reply, sitting up in the bed. The sheets are soaking wet from perspiration, and I feel the clothes sticking to my body.

I have not written my letter. The onionskin sits on the night table. I am hoping the priest will leave, but he sits at the edge of the bed and will not move. "How are you feeling, Qivitoq?"

"Much better."

"You need to be at top strength if you are to compete. I am friends with some of the best doctors in the city —"

"No doctors," I reply. "Please."

He hands me the package. "I have brought you a change of clothing. I hope everything fits."

"Thank you."

I am moved by his generosity, but by accepting the gift I am even more in debt to him, and this bothers me.

As I change clothing, he walks to the window. It is late afternoon, and the Saint Lawrence River is the color of gunmetal. From where I stand, I can see the walls of the Citadel looming steep as shelf ice. Already the priest's legs are in shadow; soon the wall will blot out the sun entirely, and I will need to turn on the gas lamp. Night begins down here in Vieux-Québec, the Old Town, while above us the rest of Quebec City is aglow.

He does not move or speak for a long time. The shadow rises to his waist and then creeps up his black shirt.

When he turns to me again, his eyes are averted. He reaches into his rear pocket and pulls out a folded newspaper article. Carefully he flattens it on my night table, and I feel the darkness closing in like a fist.

"You are not competing in the Olympics, are you?" he asks.

The clipping is from *The New York Times,* dated April 14, 1909. Its headline is *Mene Gone to Balk Peary?: Eskimo Boy's Letter to a Friend Says He Is on His Way North.* It is a brief interview with my friend Chester Beecroft — Dob.

"You are not an Indian runner," the priest continues. "You are a Polar Eskimo, from Greenland. And your name is Mene, not Qivitoq."

I read the article carefully. *"Hikup hinaa,"* I finally say.

"Beg pardon?"

"Hikup hinaa — the edge of the ice. That is where the *qivitoq* lives. He has been banished because he abandoned his family. That is the worst punishment. You see, Eskimos have no jails. To us, misery is the state of being alone. A man without a family, without a village, is as good as dead."

"You are not alone, Mene," the priest says, kneeling before my bed.

18

"My name is Minik." I close my eyes. "*Mene* is what they hear. Like every perception of us, it is incomplete. And I know what you are going to say. I am not alone because He died for me. He bore the cross up the mountain so I could live. He is my rod and my staff. My shepherd."

"Do you know Him?"

"I know a bearded, thin man with eyes like the frozen sea. He comes, like magic, across the water and promises eternal joy. Then he forsakes men, women, and children and steals the souls of everyone they love."

The priest blinks, flustered. "This is not the man I mean. I think you are getting Him mixed up with —"

"Peary?" I stand and walk directly at him, until he must step aside. Then I pull open the glass door to the balcony. "Everything is mixed up with Peary."

Although the room is on the fourth floor, we are five stories up because of the incline. Five stories will do the trick.

"Come in," the priest says. "It's cold."

"I like the cold," I reply.

The priest tightens his scarf and folds his arms. "Then I will stand with you and demand my payment."

"I have no money —"

"My payment is your story."

He is tenacious. But my task awaits.

Below us, on the brick sidewalk, people are walking home from work. I must wait for it to empty. In the meantime, I will give the priest what he wants.

When he leaves, I will act.

19

The Star Stone: August 1897

"MINIIIIIK!"

I wince. What a voice.

Aviaq is Nuktaq's adopted daughter. She is upset, as usual. Everything upsets her, and she talks too much. Although she is twelve, she has been promised to Uisaakassak in marriage, and so she thinks she is a woman and treats me like a little boy. Frankly, on the long side of seven, I am a BIG boy.

Only a big boy could have done what I did today. I have in my sealskin pouch the body of an *uppisuaq,* a snowy owl. I caught it near the cliffs on the other side of the island. Peary has promised a knife to the first child who catches one. And I, being the best hunter of all, have won!

"MINIK," Aviaq screams, "I HAVE SOMETHING TO TELL YOU!"

I hide behind a rock outcropping and peer out. Beyond Aviaq, at the top of a steep hill, my father, Nuktaq, and Peary are deep in conversation. Henson is translating as some of Peary's men dig a trench around a familiar hulking black stone. Aviaq, to my good fortune, runs off to look for me. Maybe she will get lost. She does not know the lay of this island well.

Saiksiivik is a sacred place, full of danger and mystery, where a spirit once hurled the largest of three magic stones down from the sky. Star stones, we call them — made of iron, too heavy to be moved by anyone. Two were shaped like a woman and a dog, the third like a tent, or *tupik*. My parents and their ancestors chipped tools and weapons from the stones' dense hides and in gratitude treated them with great respect. But those weapons were crude and lumpy compared to our new *qallunaaq* knives and guns, so we have less use for the stones.

Now Peary wants to take them home. Why would he need them? No one knows. But he has become obsessed with the idea.

Qallunaaqs, I have decided, are very strange.

Before Peary, only one other person ever tried to move a star stone, an Eskimo hunter who took the head of the Woman. On his way home, the ice broke under the weight, killing him.

Already, on a previous visit, Peary succeeded in taking the Woman and the Dog to his land. According to Henson, Peary plans to push Tupik down the hill and onto the ship. My father thinks Peary's good fortune is due to run out. He is afraid the entire team will disappear into the sea.

I am afraid I might miss seeing it happen.

Peary's men have finished digging their trench and have loaded it with several black machines, one-hundred-ton

21

hydraulic jacks with flat heads. The heads have been placed flush against Tupik's sides.

At a signal from Peary, they begin to pound Tupik furiously.

POCK-POCK-POCK-POCK-POCK!

I howl with laughter at the wonderful scene. All around us is noise, noise, noise. Even Peary's ship, the *Hope,* is making a racket down in the bay. It is very close to the shore. On its deck is a big, grease-covered contraption that sends out long cables, which run over the ship's gunwales, across a small makeshift bridge, and up the steep hill to the pounding machines.

I watch, fascinated. As I step into the open, the stone tilts upward, yielding to the relentless machines. Slowly it rises from the hole and lands on its side. The earth shakes, and the stone presses into the hard frozen ground like a footprint in the snow, crumbling the rocks beneath it into dust.

The men cheer. With renewed energy, they quiet the jacks and reposition them against Tupik, preparing to push it down to the ship.

Peary's daughter, Marie, dances around her grinning father. As I approach, dragging my pouch, she waves to me and points to Tupik. In her invented "Eskimo" language she blurts out, "Ah . . . nee . . . gee . . . toe!"

Peary barks a little laugh. "Ah-ni-ghi-to," he repeats. And then, gesturing to Tupik, he shouts out: "AH-NI-GHI-TO!"

The men salute the stone. "AHNIGHITO!" they bellow — and Tupik has gained a new name.

"Piuli!" I call out, dragging my sack behind me. "Look what I —"

But I am ambushed from behind by Aviaq. "MINIK! Where have you been? I have to talk to you!"

"Leave me alone!" I cry out. "Talk to Uisaakassak!"

Aviaq does not like when I mention Uisaakassak. He is twenty-one, almost twice her age. "That ugly walrus," she says. "He drools over me. But he won't be able even to *look* at me when I'm all the way across the ocean, in Siliksi . . . Sivikvee . . ."

She runs over to Henson, taps him on the shoulder, and repeats the name.

"Civilization," he corrects her.

"Yes!" Aviaq says, smiling smugly. "That is the name of Peary's land. Now Eqariusaq and I will be the only two who have gone there!"

No one, *no one,* can make me angrier than Aviaq.

She is lying. She is saying this just to make me angry. Ever since Peary took Aviaq's sister to his land two years ago, I've dreamed of going, too. Eqariusaq is as shy as Aviaq is loud, but little by little she has told me tales: Ships that travel on land and under the earth, without sails or oars. Igloos stacked high as icebergs, moving boxes that take people up and down. Winter days full of sun. Ground soft as fur.

I turn over my sack and let the enormous owl slide to the ground. "You see this? *I* am the best hunter. *I* am the one Peary should take. I can help him find food in his land! Why does he need some loud girl?"

23

Aviaq protests, but her voice is drowned out as the machines start up again. I grab the owl and drag it along the ground toward Peary. "Look . . . Piuli, *uppisuaq!* PIULIII! MAHRI-PAHLUK! LOOK!"

As I pass Ahnighito the workers smile, nodding their approval. From halfway down the hill my father shouts congratulations. I wave to them all like a triumphant hero. But the look in Peary's eyes stops me cold. He yells something in English, and Henson comes running. The two men stoop to pick up the owl.

Muttering, Peary turns back to his work.

"Thank you, Minik," Henson says in our language, placing the owl gently on a rock. "This will be valuable to us. Our people have never seen one of these."

"Piuli doesn't like it?" I ask.

"He is concerned that you dragged it, but I think the feathers can be cleaned. You are a fine hunter."

"Yes — and Aviaq cannot hunt!" I blurt out. "So take *me* with you when you go!"

"Minik —" Aviaq shouts.

"MINIK, THE STRONG HUNTER!" My father scoops me up and swings me around. "Have you heard? Piuli has chosen the best two workers to go with him — and Nuktaq will be taking his whole family."

"Two workers?" I repeat. "Who is the other?"

My father draws himself to his full height, which is just about up to Mahri-Pahluk's collarbone. "Me."

I look from my father to Nuktaq to Mahri-Pahluk, hoping that this is a joke. "But — but you can't leave me alone!"

24

Aviaq bursts out laughing. I lunge after her, but my father pulls me back. "Of course I can't," he says. "You're going with us!"

I am stunned. I cannot speak.

I leap into his arms. Then I jump down and begin running around like a crazy person, tapping on Ahnighito, dancing, making everyone around me laugh.

Everyone but Peary, that is. As I begin dancing with one of his shovels, I hear him shout my name.

He approaches me, his stiff steps heavy in the gravel and snow. In his right hand is a knife.

I scream.

He is going to kill me.

Inussuarana?

"It was rusted and old," I say.

"What was?" The priest is with me on the balcony. A stiff breeze is blowing in from the river.

"The knife," I reply. "It was my reward for catching the owl. I thought Peary was trying to murder me."

"You don't like him — Peary."

"Robert Peary is a leader of men. He gives them what they need and asks for their lives in return."

"An explorer cannot accomplish anything by being timid."

I turn to face him. "Accomplish what? The conquest of something that doesn't exist?"

"He is on his way to the North Pole. He has instruments that can measure —"

"The top of the earth is sea ice. It moves. If he plants a flag on what he thinks is the pole, it will soon after be chewed on by huskies in Siberia."

I glance below us.

Five stories.

The crowd is thinning. Soon it will be gone.

The priest takes my arm. "Perhaps you need to rest more. It has been a long struggle for you. Certainly you must be experiencing feelings of . . . melancholia."

"Melancholia?"

"I have read about you, Mene . . . Minik. Your road has been difficult. When a child is taken from his home against his will, to a place like New York City —"

I laugh. "Against my will? I was *excited!* When Peary brought Eqariusaq back, I made her tell me *everything.* Her descriptions made no sense — how do you imagine a tree when you have never seen one? But they gave me a wild desire to see New York. She warned me against going. She said that I would return a different person. For the rest of my life, she said, I would always think about this wonderful world, which I can never call home. And it would break my heart."

"Was she right?"

"Not in the way I expected." My eyes follow a schooner tacking on the river, leaving a trail like the stroke of a paintbrush.

"How, then?"

He is trying to distract me. I fear he knows I have something planned and wants me back inside.

On the sidewalk below I see a dull glow. I lean farther and focus my eyes as a figure takes form within the light. I blink once. Twice.

It is my father.

He has found me!

Standing alone on the sidewalk, he makes seal motions and funny faces. He breaks into a laugh and I laugh with him. Then he gestures to the east, mouthing *"Attuuk! Attuuk!"* I look up the street, past the café. Perhaps he is warning me of people approaching, telling me that I should hurry.

But I cannot act now. Not with the priest by my side. I must be alone.

Beside me, the priest stiffens. "Minik, *how* was your friend wrong?" he says, edging closer.

I turn to face him. His eyes are deep brown, probing. They are the eyes of an educated man, one who weighs considerations, who respects reason over instinct, like Dob and Uncle Will.

Salvation, they believe, can be found in science and symbols. They cannot possibly understand what I see, *how* I see.

"Eqariusaq had it backward," I say. "She was lured and dazzled, yes. But when she left, her heart wasn't broken. It was only wounded, like a bird's injured wing. Back home, it was able to mend. You see, it is only when you *stay* — when you cannot return to your real home — that your heart truly breaks."

It is time now. It is time for the priest to go.

I feign sudden faintness and let the priest help me back into the room. As he sets me on the bed, he seems relieved. "Perhaps a hearty meal will make you feel better," he suggests, shutting the glass door behind him. "The café below —"

28

"I have no appetite," I reply. "I'll sleep now and eat to-morrow. I'm so sorry I have spoiled your plans."

"No trouble at all."

The priest waits a few minutes while I pretend to doze off. Then he tiptoes out of the room, leaving the door ajar.

When I hear his footsteps reach the bottom of the stairs, I swing out of bed.

Grabbing the pen, I write a short note to the priest. *I will always be grateful for your kindness. Minik.*

I grab the glass doors, but they are stuck. The priest, somehow, has locked them. Mustering up all my strength, I give the door frame a kick.

The doors open in a shower of breaking glass. I step onto the balcony and glance below.

My father has waited. His arms are still open.

"*Inussuarana?*" I call out. Are you man or spirit?

He answers, but I cannot understand.

We are in two worlds, he and I. In his, he seems whole and happy. He is dead but alive. I am alive but dead.

I put one foot on the railing and prepare to join him.

Ataata

"Over here! *Vite! Vite!*"

To my left, men race out of the café. I hear metal and china clattering to the sidewalk as they pull cloths off the tables. In an instant they are below me, spreading a makeshift white net.

In the place where my father stood a moment ago, the priest directs the operation. His eyes are fixed on me. Even at this distance I can read panic in them. "Minik, my son, think about this!" he calls.

My son. The words sting.

I am bombarded from below by words. French words I don't recognize. Pleas and admonitions.

A crowd has formed out of nowhere. Patrons of the café with napkins still hanging from their trouser waists. A garishly dressed woman, no doubt the chanteuse. A balding man with waxed mustaches, suspenders, and rolled-up shirtsleeves — the piano player. An elderly couple with three small children.

They will all see me. I will either break through the cloth and splatter them or suffer the indignity of a rescue.

This is not what I had planned.

30

My father. Where is he? I look around and spot the glow, farther away now, by the river.

He gestures to his right again. *Attuk.* This time I look, seeing nothing but the faint dusky outline of Île d'Orléans.

When I turn back he is walking toward the water.

"AAA-TAAA-TAAAA!" I cry. *Father!*

He smiles over his shoulder. Then he and the glow vanish.

Where is he?

I hear a low distant moan that builds to a shrill wail. It is a moment before I realize it is my own voice.

My arms weaken. From below a cry, a collective gasp. The rumbling of assertive male voices. The priest cajoling.

I hug the railing, lying along it sideways, one leg on either side. I can stay here and rest.

Or I can tilt either way.

From inside I hear the thumping of footsteps on the stairs, the crunch of fallen glass under shoes, and I close my eyes.

A hand grasps my outside leg, another around my arm. I am lifted off the railing by two, then four, six arms. I open my eyes but cannot see the men through my tears.

They lay me on the bed. I am yelling, but my words are unconscious.

Why did I do this?

Why did I choose to stay here — to live?

The priest sits by me, swabbing my forehead with a damp hand towel, reassuring the boardinghouse's *propriè-taire,* Madame Jolliet, who paces loudly, blathering in breathless French. The men behind them congratulate one another, their voices hale and overloud with the manic energy of a disaster averted.

I look out the window, trying to see the river, to find my father. From this angle I see only the opposite shore and the grassy slope of the town called Lévis.

I have no courage.

I am not like him. Not like him at all.

My head sinks to the pillow, but the image does not leave. In my mind, on the canvas beneath my eyelids, the landscape is growing, splitting, swelling.

But I am no longer looking at Lévis and Île d'Orléans. I am no longer in Quebec City.

The balcony railing is now the gunwale of a ship; the Saint Lawrence River is Buttermilk Harbor, Brooklyn.

Kiiha Takeqihunga.

I have come.

To New York City.

Part Two
New York, September 30, 1897

Arrival

Is this what Eqariusaq meant?

Is this what a breaking heart feels like? It pounds with the fury of the jacks from Saiksiivik, with the impatience of a sled dog straining at its traces. I grip tight to the railing of the *Hope* to keep myself from shooting up into the clouds.

Can I have felt so homesick and nauseated moments ago? The storms, the humidity that has made us feel simultaneously too hot and too cold, the miserable docking in Canada where Peary departed the ship — all forgotten.

My father holds me tightly, and I hold Qunualuq, keeping his eyes trained on the shore, making sure he sees.

"Igloo, igloo, igloo, quah quah quah pah che!" says my father, over and over. So many, many, many houses.

I have never seen a building larger than Peary's hut, let alone a city. So New York seems to me at first not a place of houses and trading but an eruption of land, as if the rock itself has heaved up in a violent cataclysm to form the structures before us. They wink and dance in the changing light, all angles and thrusts, a sprawling rampart armed throughout with black spires that rise like giant arrows from quivers of stone. So densely crowded are the shapes, so varied in

35

height, that I cannot see where they touch the ground and thus assume they are all connected. Hollowed out, colonized, their walls pocked by glass, they seem too fragile for their bulk and will collapse, I'm afraid, section by section like glaciers calving from a summer-rotted ice shelf.

It is a place of stone and steel and glass, and yet it seems alive, belching smoke and noise, breathing, beckoning. It is as if the sounds of the bay — ship horns, bell buoys, sailors' shouts — are a response to the city's siren cry, a din of alluring ugliness from which there is no relief. Machines screech and howl from long warehouses that lie at odd angles to the shore like washed-up driftwood. Behind them, derricks move steadily left and right, transporting planks and beams and metal sheets to jagged, roofless structures — I cannot tell if they are half formed or half destroyed.

And that is what excites me so, although I cannot put it in words. The incompleteness of it all. New York is growing, breaking down, expanding. I can see it pushing against its limits and charging through.

It is, in the end, a child.

It is like me.

The next day, under a cloud cover like a warm glove, people gather on the dock to see us. A man with a loud, nasal voice urges them into a line and up a wooden stairway to the ship. He chants directions like a song, all the while collecting coins from each person. Anyone who can't pay twenty-five cents is sent away.

The air is thick and too warm, as it has been since we

reached Canada. After Peary disembarked, Henson allowed me to run around naked on deck. I tried that today, but a man with a bushy black mustache threw a sack over me. He told Henson that all of us Eskimos had to wear our bearskin coats for the visitors. His name is Boas. His thin, bony face and nervous manner make him seem younger than the sailors, but Henson tells us he's important like Peary.

So, sweating in the October sun, we stand in a line — Nuktaq, Atangana, Aviaq, my father, and me. Uisaakassak, having threatened to kill himself in Greenland if Aviaq left without him, is with us, too. He proposes marriage to the first five women we meet. They smile and nod, not understanding a word, but Aviaq smacks him anyway and he finally stops.

We have learned a new English phrase, which we say whenever someone gives us candy or peanuts:

"TANK YOU!"

"TANK YOU!"

We're not told what this means, but we say it gladly because, judging from the results, we assume it is English for "MORE CANDY AND PEANUTS!" I am convinced it is the only phrase I will ever need to learn. I especially love chocolate.

Everyone is tall. They file past us, chortling like contented birds. The women smell of biscuits, the men of smoke, and they are so confined by buttons and hooks that I wonder how they put on their clothes each day. Some of them, who daub their faces with white handkerchiefs, have red eyes and wet noses like my mother did when she was sick.

They are also unpredictable, like the thin man with

walrus whiskers who examines me through a monocle. I yelp at the sight of his distorted eye, and he laughs like a seal. So I imitate him, clapping my hands for effect — "Arr! Arr!" — which angers him but amuses his wife. Although she is big enough to stop a charging musk ox, she offers me her hand with exceeding daintiness. I pull off her glove, thinking candy is hidden inside it. When she recoils, her hoopskirt bells suddenly outward — and I wonder if her body conforms to the skirt's bulbous shape. So I lift it to look. This causes her to run off in a huff, but her husband chuckles and hands me three pennies, which I try to eat but spit out because they hurt my teeth.

"TANK YOU!"

This sort of thing continues throughout the day. By noon my hand is sore. My stomach, bloated with sweets, is making noises. Soon I forget my new words, but it doesn't seem to matter, because when I speak Eskimo — "You have a face like a walrus. . . . You smell like dead auks. . . . Who passed gas? . . ." — they beam with satisfaction, as if I am complimenting their wardrobe. Aviaq is laughing, and so is Uisaakassak. But I am becoming sicker and sicker, until I stop speaking altogether. And soon I feel my father's hand in mine, pulling me away.

We make our way belowdecks. It is darker and cooler there, and we sit in the hold, by Ahnighito.

"Rest," my father says.

The timbers below the stone are warped and cracking. I imagine my stomach to be the same way. "Am I going to die?" I ask.

My father assures me I won't, fanning me with a sheaf of papers he's found on a barrelhead. "When news of the birth of Piuli's daughter reached us," he says, "his men celebrated. They offered me a food they had made, soft and sticky. If you ate one piece, you had to have another. They gave me a drink, too. It made all my pain vanish into happiness, and I had to have more. I thought, *These* are what we need during our long winter — this food, made of dust and water, for which no one has to hunt! This drink, which brings strength in a few gulps! All of it had such great magic.

"The morning after the party, I was so sick I could not move. The *qallunaaqs* themselves were fine. Laughing at me! I thought, Ah well, each to his own magic. Theirs works for them, ours for us — and trying to exchange will only lead to bad luck. This is a good lesson for you, Minik."

I think about this. "What about their guns and knives and tools? We took their best magic! All they took was our stone. That was good for us."

My father pats Ahnighito's side. "Yes, but now we depend on them. Imagine if they stop visiting us. If we lose their guns, if we run out of bullets or knives or tools — then what? Ahnighito is now theirs!"

"Do you think they will stop visiting us?"

"Piuli wants to journey to the top of the world. But how will he know where it is? He will either find it, convince himself he has found it, give up, or die in the effort. No matter which happens, the *qallunaaqs* will stop coming. And we will be on our own."

"Then we will all come here and eat chocolate!" I declare,

letting out a burp so loud that my father falls over in mock horror.

"The call of the giant belching seal! I must catch him!"

I yelp and run away. But my foot catches on a plank and I fall against one of the barrels. It tips over and we both lunge for it.

But we are too late. The lid falls off, and out spill the barrel's contents.

Bones. Dozens of them.

"Quickly, let's clean up," my father says, setting the barrel upright as I begin to scoop up the spill.

The bones are odd — larger than those of a fish or an Arctic hare, smaller than a bear's. "What are these?" I ask.

"The *qallunaaqs* have many creatures, many sizes."

"But how can they be taking *their* creatures from *our* land?"

Uisaakassak's bellowing voice calls to us from above-decks. Mr. Boas is wondering where we are.

"You ask too many questions, little one," my father says. "They have customs. Maybe they carry the bones back and forth. Now hurry!"

He waits, holding the lid, as I throw in an armful of bones.

But before he closes the barrel for good, I catch a glimpse of something inside. A skull.

If it is a *qallunaaq* creature, it is very similar to a human being.

Thirty Thousand Hands

We never speak of the bones again. We are too busy.

In two days, thirty thousand people visit us. They begin to look alike. I begin to suspect they are the same few, circling around to the back of the line to visit again. After a while we stop shaking hands. We stop smiling, too — except for my father, who is, after all, called Smiler. And, of course, Qunualuq.

When we are finally taken ashore, we are so delighted we can hardly stop talking. Mr. Boas leads us into a horse-drawn carriage and we ride into Manhattan over the Brooklyn Bridge. To us, its stanchions and cables are like masts and halyards of a ship so enormous that it has become stuck sideways in the river.

We call Mr. Boas "the Scratcher," because he is always taking notes. He can speak some Eskimo words, but it is a dialect of a Canadian tribe, which is hard for us to understand. Mostly he speaks English, and Henson translates.

The carriage takes us through streets clogged with men and women, vigorous and lame, purposeful and inert. Children play unrecognizable games, deftly avoiding piles of refuse in the street. Dogs, skinny and short furred, bark senselessly at us. So do some of the people. The igloos are like walls of a fjord, and I cannot look at their roofs for fear that they will fall on us. Like the *qallunaaqs* themselves, they have first names — Tower, Cable, Crocker, Park Row, Saint Paul — but they share the same last name, Building. On a wide track called Broadway, great boxes move on wheels, pulled by nothing, over silver runners embedded in the street. I admire what appear to be two long bridges on either side of the street, until I hear the sudden roar of an elevated train, which is like the end of the world.

Farther north the countryside is sparser, some of the land rocky like Greenland, some green and fragrant. I learn that *qallunaaqs* can make food grow in the ground, which makes me look in vain for people eating trees. Everything — the farms, the houses, the pastures — is jammed together into straight, square blocks. People must travel in straight lines, even if diagonal or curved would be more direct. This makes them quiet and sad looking, so I wave and make funny faces at everyone.

We are taken to a massive stone igloo standing alone in a place called the West Side. The nearest buildings seem to be shunning it, clustered far away behind an elevated track. I nickname the igloo *Qivitoq Building*. I will not be able to pronounce its real name — the New York Museum of Natural History — for quite some time.

We are taken to the basement and given a room there. On the positive side, I am at last in a place where I can take off my clothes and run around. On the negative side, I am told by a woman named Margaret that I must sit in a bathtub with water as warm as spit.

"It is Mr. Jesup's request," Henson explains. Mr. Jesup is the leader of the museum. I have not met him, but I dislike him already.

My father, Uisaakassak, and Nuktaq's family take baths first. Afterward they smell like the ladies who greeted us aboard the *Hope*.

I am last, alone in the room with Margaret. I try to reason with her. "I will not go in!" I say in Eskimo. "But if you take me to the sea . . ."

She tries to edge closer, holding a brush and a towel. I circle the tub, keeping it between us. When her back is to the wall, mine is to the door — and I run.

My footsteps slap on the cement floor of the dark basement hallway. The coolness is refreshing. I look for a place to hide, but most of the doors are locked. At the end of the hall I see an open room. But inside it is a man draping a skin over a frame, trying to re-create an animal.

I watch him for a moment, baffled. "Why did you skin it in the first place?" I ask.

"SMILER!" comes Margaret's voice, shouting for my father.

I sprint around a corner and see a grating above me. This means I am near our living quarters. Museumgoers come to the grating to peer at us. Lying on their stomachs, they wave to us and drop scraps of food.

"Hel-lo! Hel-lo! Tank you!" I call to the faces pressed to the metal, using my entire English vocabulary.

My father, Nuktaq, Uisaakassak, and Atangana are at a table, trying to eat *qallunaaq* food. Uisaakassak is hooting with laughter. My father lifts me and puts me over his shoulder. His hair is shiny and seems a lighter color.

"Don't let her touch me!" I cry.

Margaret charges around the corner with her towel. I am bouncing on my father's shoulder, and I realize he is coughing.

She is now breathless, complaining to him in English. He nods, as if he understands. He will do anything to please her. That is his way. That is *our* way.

At the moment, however, it is not my way.

"Minik, we will stay with you while you are in the water," says my father. "It is their custom."

I am forced back toward the bathroom, screaming and pulling my father's hair.

The people behind the grating have gotten quite a show.

We are fast becoming famous. The next day an article appears in *The New York Times,* a mix of odd perceptions and outright lies that I save for the rest of my life.

Kushu's little son, of unspellable and unpronounceable name, but called Minny for short, was happy in the possession of a knickerbocker suit and blue flannel waist, which he took great delight in exhibiting to callers, his chubby, greasy, little face beaming with delight at his civilized appearance. For the first time in his life, probably, he had a real bath yesterday, and, though it took some coaxing to get him to enter the

44

tub of water, after the performance was over, he was so pleased that he has been anxiously inquiring through Matthew Henson, the colored interpreter, when the next bath was forthcoming.

We Are Home: February 1898

"The sleepy walrus opens his eyes. . . ."

My father's voice is the first sound I hear in the morning. As always, he sits by my bed and waits for me to waken.

We have been in New York for more than four months. I am seven years old, perhaps eight; it is hard to know. Much of the time we have all been sick — and I am convinced the bathwater caused it. We've spent much time in and out of Bellevue Hospital, where the doctors have fed us foul liquids and smothered us with wet, hot towels. But good things have happened, too. We have met Uncle Will — William Wallace, the museum superintendent. And he has moved us to our new, large rooms on the sixth floor.

Uisaakassak is still asleep on the floor. He dislikes beds.

I know that the sun has risen, because I see it reflected in my father's eyes. He helps me up and puts my face to the open window. The air is cold, and snow is falling heavily. Lately the weather has been welcome.

"Ready?" he asks.

"Ready," I reply.

We both squint.

"See it?"

"Yes!"

Together we shout: "Look . . . WE ARE HOME!"

This is our game, now that we are in new quarters in the museum. Our windows face east, across Central Park. Beyond the leafless trees is a small, iced-over lake. If you squint and use a lot of imagination, the light's reflection off the water, along with the white landscape, resembles our village on Smith Sound.

"Today —" my father begins. But his voice catches, and he begins coughing. I have gotten used to this. He has been coughing for almost four months, since late October. I have noticed lately that the sound has changed. It is drier, more rattly. "Today," he continues, "Mr. Wallace will take us to the circus."

I yelp with excitement. I love the circus at Madison Square Garden. Mr. Wallace has taken us there twice already. It is a long ride from the museum, but Mr. Wallace believes that "fresh air" is good for our health. Of all the *qallunaaqs,* he is one I have grown to like most. He is quiet and patient, with a shy smile and an open, oval-shaped face that reminds me of a curious Arctic seal. In his creaky horse-drawn carriage we have been through all of Central Park and the West Side and along both rivers. But the circus is my favorite. I have a friend there, an elephant named Hilda who has a pointy head and a notch in her left ear. On our first visit she swiped an entire bag of peanuts out of my hand. While the others moved on to watch the clowns, jugglers, and animal tricks, I stayed with Hilda. The afternoon feeding her peanuts was one of the happiest of my life.

We meet often with men who seem to be in competition for Mustaches That Most Resemble a Broom. The winners appear to be Mr. Jesup and his friend, a gentle giant named Herbert Bridgman. Occasionally two scientists named Kroeber and Hrdlicka observe us. But we like the Scratcher, Mr. Boas, the best. He takes great interest in what we do. He shows us fossils in the rock; he has also let us use binoculars and telescopes, and he has taken photographs of us all. I carry the image of my father and me wherever I go. The Scratcher grew very excited on the day that Nuktaq and Uisaakassak built a small igloo in the park after a snowstorm. But when he found out they intended to live in it, he had a fit. Nuktaq and Uisaakassak slept in the museum that night but sneaked out the next day, only to find that the igloo had been smashed and scattered about.

Sometimes the Scratcher tries our patience. He took notes when Atangana performed a shaman ritual on my father to improve his health. As she massaged his sides, chanting for the intervention of the helping *toorngat*, Mr. Boas had the audacity to ask her to repeat herself. My father became sicker, and so did Atangana. The only one who didn't get sick was the Scratcher.

"Mr. Boas is studying you," Henson says. "He wants to find out how you live and work. How you talk to one another. Our people have never seen Greenland Eskimos. We have much to learn."

Atangana wants to learn, too. She wants to know why the *toorngat* have abandoned us.

Today, though, I am certain things will change. The snow is making us all happy. I am about to kick Uisaakassak to wake him when he sits up suddenly from his pallet on the floor.

"She is talking about me!" he exclaims.

My father and I exchange a glance. Then, from the room next door, where Nuktaq and his family are staying, I hear giggles.

"You heard that in your sleep?" I ask.

"If his name is mentioned, he hears it across the world," my father says.

Uisaakassak shuffles silently to a table and picks up an empty drinking glass. He places the open end against the wall between the rooms. Then he puts his ear to the base of the glass.

"What are you doing?" my father asks.

"Mr. Boas taught me to do this," Uisaakassak replies. "I am listening. Sound goes through glass."

"Perhaps Atangana can sew the glass onto your ear, so you will never miss another word," my father says. Then, turning to me, he adds, "Are you ready to visit Hilda?"

I jump on the bed with delight. I extend my arm in front of my face like an elephant's trunk and make a trumpet noise. Uisaakassak quickly grows tired of listening to the wall, puts down the glass, and jumps on the bed with me. He is imitating me, trumpeting and giggling, which makes me laugh and jump even more. Our combined weight sends the bed sliding across the wooden floor.

"Careful, little one!" my father warns.

Screaming with glee, I tumble off the bed and into his outstretched arms.

He catches me. And then he collapses.

I hear the thud of his head against the floor. His eyes close. When I yell out, Uisaakassak stops jumping. "GET MAHRI-PAHLUK!" I shout.

Mr. Wallace, whose office is on the fifth floor, is there in an instant. Mr. Boas is right behind him. I watch them carry my father away. Nuktaq tries to help, but he tips and falls down the stairs. His wife and daughter have to help him to his feet.

A wagon has pulled into the circular driveway on West Seventy-seventh Street. The doctor helps put my father on a cot inside. He takes a look at the rest of us and orders us to climb in, too.

Quickly the horses pull us across the park. The transverse road at West Eighty-first Street is cut through solid granite. Dark and ominous in the daylight, it feels like a tunnel into the underworld. When my father's eyes flutter open, he seems confused and scared until he sees me.

"Ready?" he says, clutching my hand. I see his eyes slowly closing again. "Look, Minik . . . we are home!"

On February 17th, my father is dead.

High Bridge

"You will bury me, Nuktaq?" she wails. "You will not let them take me?"

I am riding in the front seat of a large carriage up Broadway. Behind me, Atangana is moaning. Her neck is swollen, too, the way my father's became before he died. Nuktaq tends to her, softly reassuring her that everything will be all right.

Her cries barely register with me. I take no notice of the automobiles or the horses or the shouting of the newsies. I do not feel the freezing rain that has begun to fall lightly, wetting Mr. Boas's photograph of my father and me, which I clutch tightly. I am numb to all feeling.

I am, as a newspaper called me, the Orphan Mene.

"At night, Minik, these theaters are bright as fire." The Scratcher is translating for Mr. Wallace, who is trying to cheer me up, pointing out and describing all the sights. "The Knickerbocker, the Empire, the Casino, and the great Metropolitan Opera House . . . and here is Longacre Square, which is becoming the new theater district. . . ."

Unconsciously I rub the burn mark on my left forearm. The day before my father died, I played a trick on one of the

51

doctors. While the doctor was using a hot iron, I sneaked up behind him and shouted, "Woola woola!" I had no good reason to do this. I was fearful, I suppose, and full of energy. The doctor turned, startled, and inadvertently burned me with the iron. Later that day, when my father saw the burn mark, he pulled himself out of bed. "Who did that to you?" he demanded. "I will kill him!"

I was afraid for the doctor. It took a lot to get Smiler angry, and I knew that look in my father's eyes. "It is nothing," I said, gently pushing him back to bed. "I touched a gas lamp." The outburst left him exhausted. He sank onto the mattress. His neck was swollen. He smiled, as always, but I saw a blackness in his eyes, a terror that distorted his face. For a long time he tried to speak. Then he signaled me to come closer and whispered, "Father's spirit will stay with Minik always."

Those were his last words. He died that night, while I was sleeping. When I awoke, his body was gone.

I have thought about those words every minute of every day. I've tried to feel that spirit but have felt nothing but guilt. If I had done something different, would the spirits have let him live longer? If I hadn't lied to him, if I hadn't scared the doctor and gotten burned, if I hadn't jumped into my father's arms that morning at the museum . . .

"Minik, you can't send the snow back into the clouds," Nuktaq told me. He also assured me that he would command Mr. Boas to bury my father properly, so his spirit would not haunt me, monstrous and angry.

52

But I don't know if Nuktaq has done that. With Atangana's sickness, he has a lot on his mind. I believe he is trying to send some snow back himself.

"Just ahead, beyond the carriage-sale district here, we will see your favorite place, Central Park," the Scratcher says.

I take little notice of the park, which vanishes into the distance anyway as we travel up Broadway. It seems like days later when we finally turn east along Kingsbridge Road around the scraggly granite ridges of Upper Manhattan. As we approach the Harlem River, a one-masted bridge of gleaming silver appears. Mr. Wallace beams when he sees our reactions, as if he had built it himself. "The Macombs Dam Bridge," he explains, through Mr. Boas. "Two years old, solid steel. I live across the river, a mile or so north, in an area named for a rich man, Jonas Bronck. When you traveled this far, you said you were visiting the Broncks."

Mr. Wallace's house is large and tidy, on a well-kept piece of land near a steep bluff. It overlooks yet another structure, the High Bridge, which carries water to Manhattan over tremendous stone arches. In back of the house is a small cottage. A sled, some animal skins, and various Eskimo tools have been set out front.

A plainly dressed woman with sad wide-set eyes emerges from the big house. "This is Mrs. Wallace," says Mr. Boas. "She welcomes you to your new home."

I head to the cottage, but I am stopped by a banana hurtling by my face from the right.

I see a pair of eyes and a head of blond hair in a first-floor window of Mr. Wallace's house. They belong to a boy about my age. He makes a monkey face, sticks out his tongue, and sinks below the sill.

"Willie!" shouts Mrs. Wallace.

Mr. Wallace looks angry. He says something to Mr. Boas, who tells us, "Excuse Willie. He will be punished."

Eqariusaq and Aviaq rush into the cottage. Behind them, Nuktaq and Uisaakassak carefully help Atangana. I follow them in. There is a living room (which contains a small kitchen), two small bedrooms, and a bathroom. The beds have fluffy pillows and soft white covers with tassels along the bottom. Nailed to the wooden walls are paintings of Arctic scenes. Glaciers, fjords, dogsleds, igloos.

Through the window I hear raised voices. They are coming from a shed behind the big house. I hear a dull slap and a boy's voice cries out in pain.

From the pocket of my coat I take out my doll, Qunualuq, and the photograph of my father and me.

I sit on my bed, holding them close. And I don't move all night.

The Burial

"Ashes to ashes, dust to dust . . ."

On a cold night in late February, the wind whips eddies of dust across the empty lot behind the museum. I do not understand the words of the man in black, but I assume he is there for the *qallunaaqs*. They have their own rituals.

I stand silently with Mrs. Wallace, whom I now call Aunt Rhetta. Through my grief, I am nonetheless relieved. Mr. Boas has agreed — and remembered — to bury my father.

The silhouette of the museum's north tower is black against the approaching night. Four men emerge from the door — Uncle Will, Mr. Boas, and two others I do not know. On their shoulders they carry a box, open at the top, which contains my father.

I expect them to remove him from the box and place him on the ground. Instead they set the box in a hole, about four feet deep, near a pile of stones. As it is lowered I can see inside. My father is wrapped in the skin of a bear, head to toe. I look for his possessions, which must be buried with him. He did not bring much to New York — some small weapons and tools — but none of them are with him.

"An Eskimo man must have something to carry into the spirit world!" I say to Aunt Rhetta in Eskimo, but of course she cannot understand. I pull my Qunualuq from my coat. He is mine, not my father's, yet when I see one, I see the other. I want to bury them together.

I try to run forward, but Aunt Rhetta pulls me back. She holds my hand tightly. Her palm is cold, and she is crying.

"*Naan!*" I cry out. No!

I break loose and run toward my father, but one of the men lifts me off my feet and holds me aloft, kicking and crying.

So much of what they are doing is wrong — the hole, the box, *why won't they take him out of the box?* I think of the burial ritual for my mother. The things my father said to her body. The way he dressed her. Am I supposed to do these things for him? I am only eight. I don't know enough. I would get it all wrong. Nuktaq would know, or Atangana. But they were too sick to come tonight; Uncle Will would not allow them.

The man gives me to Aunt Rhetta, who holds me as I sob. There is so much I want to tell her but can't. I will learn English. I vow I will learn it faster than anyone ever has. Then Aunt Rhetta will know.

The men place the box on the ground so that my father's head points north, away from the museum. It should be pointing away from the sea — but where is the sea when you are on an island? South? That seems right. We came from the south.

After closing the box, the men bow their heads as the

56

priest drones on. Then they pick up stones. Mr. Boas drops the first one. It makes a hollow sound on the wood. The others begin to cover the body.

"They are hurting him!" I scream.

I *hear* him. With each stone, I hear my father cry out in pain.

"They are hurting him! He will cry and never be happy! He will come back and do bad things! THEY ARE HURTING HIM!"

I try to run forward, but Aunt Rhetta embraces me tightly. "Shhh, shhh," she says. She holds me so close I feel her heartbeat.

My shouts turn into moans. I find myself gasping for breath. Aunt Rhetta rubs my back, singing a soft song, words I cannot remember. She is crying, too.

When I look up, my father is a mound of rocks.

Mr. Boas is leaning over me now. "It is done, Minik," he says in his strange accent. "It is good now."

The men nod toward me, then head for the museum.

My father's voice has gone quiet. I wipe my face. Taking a deep breath, I pick up a stick and walk to the mound. There I turn. I must make a mark between my father's grave and my house, to protect it from evil spirits.

I imagine where Uncle Will's High Bridge house is. When I think I am facing in the right direction, north and east, I make a mark in the ground.

"Home," I say to Aunt Rhetta, using one of the only English words I know.

Alone

February 17th. My father.

March 16th. Atangana.

May 14th. Nuktaq.

May 24th. Aviaq.

I have been learning about *qallunaaq* time — seconds, minutes, days, weeks, months, years — and I have all the dates memorized.

Ninety-six days, four Eskimos. Dead, dead, dead, dead.

They call the disease *consumption,* which means the body eats itself alive. It comes from pneumonia, which starts as sneezing and coughing. It is the *qallunaaq* disease, the one that killed my mother.

The worst part of it is that I was not able to see them. When they were moved in February to Uncle Will's farm in upstate New York — to partake of the cleaner air — I was deemed too sick to travel. Since then I have been living with Mr. Jesup, the head of the museum and the president of the Peary Arctic Club.

Uisaakassak and I are the only ones left. Recently Uisaakassak visited me. He is very upset about losing Aviaq and scared of getting the disease. He says that Mr. Boas and his workers had taken all the bodies away before they could be buried properly. "All those angry spirits!" he said.

"Not my father," I told him. "My father was buried."

"How do you know it was really him?" Uisaakassak asked.

If he weren't so much bigger than me, I would have punched him.

As it turned out, Uisaakassak is the lucky one. Peary has allowed him aboard his ship, the *Windward*, docked off Canal Street. In July Uisaakassak will be gone, back to Greenland — and I will be alone.

Mr. Jesup's apartment is a dark place — dark wood walls and furniture, dark red carpets. His only pets are birds and small animals, dead and stuffed. Every morning I awaken to a portrait of Mr. Jesup's glowering face, puffed out at each side with white mustaches as thick as a rabbit's fur. I cannot do anything. I am not allowed to sleep late, to walk barefoot, to sing loudly. I cannot even be seen holding my doll, Qunualuq. Mr. Jesup does not approve of dolls for boys.

And as winter turns to spring and spring turns to summer, my fever takes hold of my body and stays. I am young enough to believe that Mr. Jesup's sudden expression of concern is about my health and not about the prospect of explaining a corpse to the public.

Then, on a cool night in June, my father comes to me in a dream.

We are hunting, sitting by a breathing hole in the ice, waiting for a seal to surface. It is summer; the sun has danced from one side of the sky to the other and is preparing to return. I am growing hungry and frustrated. Finally a snout pushes its way noisily up into the hole, and my father lifts his harpoon. But rather than killing the seal, he gives the harpoon to me.

I fumble and I hesitate, worried that I will not succeed. At my father's urging, I finally plunge the harpoon into the hole — but when I pull up, only a small fish is at the end of the hook. I throw the harpoon down in anger. The fish flies off, sliding across the ice, but my father patiently retrieves it. "How can we possibly eat this?" I ask, but my father peels it apart and hands me some of its flesh. The meat is tender and tasty. We eat and eat and eat, until my stomach is so full I cannot eat any more. Watching my reaction, my father laughs. "You see, it was a *big* fish, but you couldn't see it. Now you will never go hungry, because you didn't give up!"

When I wake up, my fever has broken. A glimmer of reflected sunlight shines through the window, and for a blissful moment I believe I am back in Smith Sound.

Until I see Mr. Jesup's portrait staring back at me through the mirror.

I sit up with a start, bumping my elbow against a night table beside my bed. On it is a bronze elephant figurine. I have taken it from Mr. Jesup's collection to remind me of my friend Hilda, whom I have begged to see for weeks.

I feel something well up inside me like the rumble of an impending avalanche. I pick up the figurine and throw it. With a crash, the mirror breaks into a shower of bright pieces.

The maid is at the door now. She screams for Mr. Jesup. I jump out of bed, running across the broken glass. It cuts my foot, but I don't care. In fact, I enjoy making footprints through the house. My feet pad across the pattern of the faded Oriental rugs. They slide across the kitchen tile. My feet. My blood. My pain. The house feels alive for the first time.

Mr. Jesup appears at the kitchen door, dressed in a floor-length gown, his head covered with a tasseled nightcap. He is holding the elephant figurine.

"What in heaven's name do you think you are you doing?" I recognize this phrase. It is one of Mr. Jesup's favorites.

I lift my injured foot. I let blood drip into the open palm of my hand. When enough has collected, I raise my hand to my mouth and I blow.

Mr. Jesup flinches. His white hair, his white mustaches, his robe, the elephant figurine — they are all flecked with red. He shrieks. His maid rushes in, still holding broken glass.

I turn to his icebox, open it, and begin pulling things onto the floor.

I cannot stop laughing.

Willie

"Raspberries," Aunt Rhetta says, holding up a handful of luscious fruit. It is July 9th, and she and Lizzie have begun preparing pies for the county fair later on.

I repeat the new word as best I can.

Willie lets out a loud hoot. "*Lazbellies?*"

Aunt Rhetta gives him the eye, and he sinks into his seat.

I have been in Lawyersville for more than two weeks, since the day I broke Mr. Jesup's mirror.

I am in debt to the Scratcher for convincing Mr. Jesup not to call the police. But that day, I had to pack up. I felt awful. I tried to apologize a hundred times to Mr. Jesup. I didn't know why I'd done those terrible things.

I still don't.

Truth to tell, though, I was relieved to be sent upstate. In Lawyersville the air is sweet with blooming flowers and cut hay. The rooms of the house are full of light. It is hot, like New York City, but a cooling breeze comes off the mountains. Uncle Will is happy to have me. He works at the museum during the week, then spends weekends here.

Aunt Rhetta and Willie are here every day. This is half

of a good thing. I am very well behaved in the house, having had no reason to break glass or such things, and Aunt Rhetta is kind to me always. She puts candy and peanuts on my bed table every morning. Willie, however, is a different story. He is nearly three years older than I am, and he will have nothing to do with me. Whenever I smile at him or try to show him something, he sneers. He plays catch with himself, throwing the ball straight up in the air. He invites friends over for tennis but doesn't let me play. So in those first days, I spend much time alone.

On the morning of July 9th, Aunt Rhetta and Lizzie, the maid, are making breakfast as usual. My favorite is sunny-side-up eggs and bacon, but today we are having porridge oats with maple syrup. I like these enough, but they always leave me hungry an hour or so later. Across the table Willie eats quickly, his right hand digging into the porridge with a spoon. In his left hand he strokes a squirrel tail. He carries this tail around with him wherever he goes.

Aunt Rhetta, continuing my English lesson, holds up a reddish stalk. "Rhubarb," she says.

I am very careful this time. "Rhu . . . barb."

This time Willie does not comment. But when his mother and Lizzie turn their backs, he smiles at me. Using his squirrel tail, he pantomimes cleaning crumbs off the table. I look up curiously, and he whispers a phrase very, very slowly.

I repeat the phrase, syllable by syllable. I want to learn it perfectly, to earn Willie's respect.

As Aunt Rhetta brings biscuits to the table I proudly

stand up, start cleaning the table, and say, "That . . . tasted . . . like . . . horse manure!"

Willie is banished to his bedroom. Howling with glee, he leaves so fast that he forgets his squirrel tail.

Lizzie and Aunt Rhetta *tut-tut* and *tsk-tsk* and apologize. But I don't mind much. I watch them shape the dough, press it into crusts, and pour in the fruit filling.

Aunt Rhetta catches my glance. "Come here, Minik," she says.

She grabs a handful of dough, squeezes it into a long strip, and places it across the top of the pie. Then she pantomimes making a crosshatch shape, explaining what the strips should look like, and she gestures for me to try.

Lizzie brings over a stool. I climb on it, and Aunt Rhetta stands behind me. As I dig eagerly into the warm, grainy dough, I feel her arms wrapping around me. She places her hands over mine. They are firm and gentle.

Together we finish the pies, laying the strips, dusting the surface with small clumps of brown sugar.

When the pies are in the oven, Lizzie applauds my effort. "Bravo!" she says.

"Bravissimo!" Aunt Rhetta echoes.

"*Poo-poo!*" calls Willie from his bedroom.

I throw my arms around Aunt Rhetta and kiss her American-style, with my lips.

Outside, the heat rises in waves from the parched grass. I can smell the pies baking as I walk away from the house for my morning exploration. In my pocket is Willie's squirrel tail, keeping Qunualuq company. I am hoping that Willie will come to me, looking for the tail, and we will become friends.

I peel off my shirt, take off my shoes, and wander along a pasture. The soft electric drone of the cicadas swells from all directions until the sound becomes suffocating, like something solid, then falls off into silence as if on cue. I pull Qunualuq from my back pocket as we pass Uncle Will's cattle. Many of them are munching grass, but even at this hour some are taking refuge in the shadows of trees. We greet Lois, the Eskimo-speaking cow. When Qunualuq asks if she's comfortable, her ears twitch and she answers, *Na-ahn!* — which means *no.*

We continue walking into a wooded area that slopes downward. I hear the rush of a brook, and as I descend, the air quickly becomes cooler.

By the brook's bank the ground is soft and springy. I set Qunualuq into a crook in a dead tree and wade into the water. A school of fish swims around me. I feel a delicious rush of cold and listen to the breeze rustling the leaves.

Up the hill, a twig cracks. I glance toward the sound, but there are no deer.

My ankle is tickled by a fat, tasty-looking fish. Despite the porridge breakfast, I feel a pang of hunger. I crouch. Frozen in position, I watch dozens of scrawny fish flitter by. When the sun glints against the multicolored scales of an approaching trout, I wait for the right moment — and I grab.

It tries to wriggle away. I feel its heartbeat, its lifeblood, against my palm. I wade quickly to the bank, splashing all the way, whispering soothing words to the fish, thanking it for its sacrifice to me. Then I knock it against a rock and pull it apart.

I have no scraping tool, so I bring the fish to my mouth and tear out the flesh with my teeth. It is smooth and delicate, cooling the insides of my cheeks. When I swallow, it feels as if the river itself is gliding down my throat.

I do not hear the footsteps behind me until it is too late. I turn to see a flash of light.

A deafening boom makes me jump backward, and the dead tree explodes into splinters.

"HOO-hahhahaha!" Willie's laugh echoes through the woods. He emerges from behind another tree, a box of matches in his hand.

I see tiny shreds of my doll on the forest floor, blackened pieces of sealskin. I lift one that has landed by the bank. It is part of the face. The smile.

My feet go forward before I have time to think. I pounce on Willie, pummeling him with my fists. He is screaming beneath me, covering his face with his hands. His eyes are wide, his mouth bloody, but all I can see is the laugh. His laugh and Qunualuq's shredded skin.

I pick up a rock, hold it over Willie's face, and plunge it down.

The Bone House

Willie rolls to the right. The rock hits the ground and I lurch forward.

He scrambles to his feet and runs. I take off after him. Willie is wearing ungainly shoes, and my bare feet cover the ground in no time. I grab for him, but my fingers close over the back pocket of his knickers. He twists away and the pocket rips in my hand.

From it spills another box of matches and firecrackers, left over from last week's July 4th celebration — the firecrackers he used to destroy Qunualuq. Why? Is it because I took his squirrel tail? Is he that cruel?

I cannot believe I ever wanted to be his friend. I pull the tail from my back pocket and throw it at him. "Yours," I say.

Willie wipes his eyes with his right hand, smearing dirt across his face. He looks surprised.

Then I show him the scrap of Qunualuq. I point to my heart. "Mine."

Willie takes the scrap and examines it. Through the blood and dirt, I can see his expression. He is surprised, remorseful. "Sorry," he says.

I realize that Willie had not seen Qunualuq. He had set off the explosion to scare me, but he hadn't intended to destroy my doll. He had been making mischief.

And I had nearly killed him.

"Sorry," I repeat.

Willie walks back to the tree stump. With a cry of triumph, he holds up another piece of Qunualuq — an arm, nearly intact — and continues searching. The idea of finding the destroyed remains makes me sad, and I cannot join him. I hike down to the brook and dangle my feet in the water.

After a while Willie kneels beside me. Leaning over, he washes the blood from his face. A school of fish flitters away from the ripples he has made.

Willie grins faintly. As another school passes, he quickly thrusts a hand into its midst. The fish easily escape. But the sudden movement makes Willie lose balance. His feet slip on a mossy rock.

With a yelp of surprise, he falls in. I laugh at first, but he does not respond.

His eyes are closed. His head has landed against a sharp rock. "Willie," I say, shaking him gently.

He doesn't respond. "WILLIE!"

In the water I see the reflection of my face, but it is twisted, ugly, evil. Evil has been growing inside me since the day at Mr. Jesup's house. I have become a killer — and I am going to have to tell Uncle Will and Aunt Rhetta.

Kneeling by Willie, I begin to cry.

He spits out a plume of water straight upward, like a whale — right into my face.

"Haaaaa-hahaha!"

Leaping from the brook, he runs into the woods. I chase him, wiping my face and laughing.

From that moment on, Willie and I are friends. We spend the rest of the afternoon meandering through Uncle Will's property. Willie offers me a cigarette, but when I try to smoke I nearly cough up my breakfast. He teaches me popular songs — "Swipsy" and "Gypsy Love Song" and "I Guess I'll Have to Telegraph My Baby." I try to teach him some of mine, too, but neither of us makes much headway.

It is early afternoon when we reach a waterfall. We clamber down a rock hill, where the brook widens into a fast-flowing river. At the bottom of the falls we skip stones until the sudden high-pitched whine of a machine pierces the stillness.

Willie takes my arm. We make our way downstream to where the river is at its widest. Perched over the water on stout wooden pylons is a large building with a smokestack. The noise, loud and insistent, is coming from within.

From behind the building, brackish white liquid spews into the brook. I watch it bubble and disperse, carrying bits of brownish material. We tiptoe around the back, and through a window I can see men working inside.

On the other side of the building, long wooden racks stretch across the lawn. They are made of slats strung with netting. Lying on them, drying in the sun, are bright white bones of all shapes and sizes — legs and arms, collars and hips. Skulls are arranged at the bottom of the racks, but I can't tell what kind of animals they belong to.

We hear voices approaching and scurry behind a thicket. At the top of the hill, an enormous horse-drawn wagon stops. Out of the back climbs a team of men, at least twenty of them. They are wearing white handkerchiefs over their mouths.

A stench wafts down as the men set to work. Some of them untether the wagon from the horses. Others unhook the walls and slide them out of their slats. On the flatbed I see a gray mass, cragged and shapeless like a boulder.

In minutes the men are carefully maneuvering the wagon toward the hill. Half of them hold on to the hitch, which is pointed uphill. The downhill half dig in their heels to keep the wagon from rolling out of control.

As they slowly descend, I see that the mass is not a boulder at all.

A boulder does not have ivory tusks. It does not have a pointy head with a notch in its big, floppy left ear.

It is Hilda.

Authentic Eskimo

"Oh, my," Uncle Will says. "Oh, you're right!"

His face is red, and he orders the men to send Hilda back. The fact that I am screaming bloody murder doesn't hurt her cause at all.

The rest of the day, Hilda's smell stays with us, but it (and she) are gone the next morning.

I mourn Hilda, even though she was an animal. When Aunt Rhetta is preparing steak that evening, I ask if the meat is Hilda, but she responds as if I have lost my mind.

As the summer progresses and my vocabulary grows, I learn about the evil little house by the brook.

It is a bone house.

A macerating plant.

You start with an animal corpse, you strip off the skin and organs, and you're left with the bones. Very useful for a museum of natural history, which needs skeletons.

It is one of Uncle Will's businesses. As I grow up with the Wallace family, I come to understand what an enterprising man he is. The macerating process requires great quantities of water, and Uncle Will convinced the museum to set up the bone house on his property, at the brook. The museum would ship bodies up to Lawyersville for treatment, and Uncle Will would earn extra income.

The incident with Hilda is the only blot on three wonderful years. I learn English rapidly and begin to earn good grades at the school that Willie attends in the Bronx. We spend summers upstate. On Sundays Uncle Will and Aunt Rhetta take me to the Reformed Church of Lawyersville, which I have deemed a boring and unnecessary place. Willie and I both try to avoid it as much as possible, and sometimes we succeed in sneaking away.

But by the summer of 1900, something has happened to Uncle Will. He has become more and more agitated, and he punishes Willie at the slightest transgression. One sweltering Sunday in late August, after a row about something petty at home, Willie and I suffer silently in the pews, trussed up in our starchy Sunday clothes. On the bright side, it is the day of the county fair, and we are counting the minutes.

In the midst of the sermon I overhear Uncle Will talking with Aunt Rhetta about Robert Peary.

I think about Peary whenever I am in church. He seems to be everywhere. The paintings of somber Saint George, long-suffering Jesus, and imperious God Himself — for the first few services I'd assumed that they were images of Peary and that everyone was worshipping *him*. But lately he has been especially on my mind. I am becoming homesick for Greenland. I am certain he will be returning north, and I hope he will offer to take me with him.

"Is Piuli in New York?" I ask Aunt Rhetta.

"It is Pea-rrrry," Aunt Rhetta says, gently correcting my pronunciation. "And no, he is not here."

I feel an elbow in my ribs. Willie is shaking his head, telling me to be quiet. After the service, as we exit the church, he and I run down the stairs. At the bottom Willie takes me around the back of the building.

We crouch in an alley between the church and the parish house. I hear a familiar voice — the Scratcher. Out front, Mr. Boas is talking to Uncle Will.

Their voices are muffled. It is not like the other church conversations, jaunty and polite. Uncle Will sounds prickly. Mr. Boas's responses are clipped and forceful.

The conversation is cut short when Uncle Will calls out, "Rhetta! Minik! Willie! Let's go. Right now."

Willie and I race back around the building. Straightening out our clothes, we emerge from the other side, where the carriage is waiting.

Uncle Will is tense throughout the ride to the county fair. I assume he and Mr. Boas have had a disagreement, but Mr. Boas is following right behind us in another carriage.

The somber mood lifts as we approach the yellow-and-white tents in a large field on the outskirts of town. I have never been to the fair before. As we ride through a high wooden arch, I see marvelous rides, clowns, jugglers, men on stilts, tables piled with baked foods — even an elephant.

But our carriage keeps going until we reach a seating area at the far end of the fair. There the crowd seems to be especially friendly. They shout and wave to us, and I wave back.

73

We stop at a wooden platform stage. Across the back is a long painting of a snowy landscape — on one side a crude polar bear waving hello, on the other a tiny domed dwelling that resembles an igloo made of ice. It is about waist high, with a smooth domed top. A group of very short, dark people in fur coats stand around it. They face the bear, some of them taking aim with enormous feathered arrows. Behind them a seal and a penguin watch, looking scared.

In letters painted to look like icicles, the title MENE, AUTHENTIC ESKIMO FROM GREENLAND is painted across the top.

People begin to applaud. Uncle Will looks a little uncomfortable, but Aunt Rhetta takes my hand and leads me onto the stage. She speaks a few words to the crowd and everyone falls silent. Then she turns to me, touches her lips, and holds her hand out flat.

I am supposed to speak. But what am I supposed to say?

The crowd begins clapping, in rhythm. My heart is pounding. I feel dizzy and stifling hot. A little girl in the second row is pointing at me and laughing. A boy from the back throws a corncob on the stage.

Willie races to the boy, but the boy's father stops him with a glare.

From the back of the crowd steps Mr. Boas. He is holding my fur coat. Leaping onto the stage, he helps me put it on, to a round of cheers. "Sing," he says.

I clear my throat and sing the first song that comes to mind. A song that has stayed with me since I was a child.

"Aya-ya-ya, aya-ya-ya,
Spirit of the sea,
Come forth with your wings and take us away,
To the place where light and dark come every day:
Where no one starves and no one suffers,
And no one is happy. . . ."

A Crooked Man

A month later I am sitting with Uncle Will in Mr. Jesup's office at the New York Museum of Natural History. I have not been here in months, but I recognize the close, musty smell of tobacco, old wood, New York City grime, and peppermint foot liniment. A recent addition, the head of a moose, glowers at us from above the fireplace.

"Morris likes to keep images of himself everywhere," says Uncle Will drily. It is his first attempt at humor in a long time.

Mr. Jesup is nowhere to be seen, even though he has summoned Uncle Will for a 10:00 A.M. Saturday meeting. I begged to come along. I want everyone at the museum to hear how well I speak English and see how much like a New Yorker I have become in manner and dress.

Uncle Will's hands knead the brim of his hat. He looks nervous and sad. He has been this way since the fall. Whenever Aunt Rhetta asks him what is the matter, he forces a smile and says he is "just woolgathering."

I believe he has gathered enough wool to clothe all of the West Side.

"Is that a moose?" I say.

"Very good," Uncle Will answers. "And the plural is . . . ?"

"Meese?" I think a moment. "No, moose."

Mr. Jesup's elephant figurine — the one I mistreated at his apartment — is now sitting on his office windowsill. I lift it to the morning light, high above the soaring rooftops across West Eighty-first Street. Two new apartment buildings are under construction, rising higher than the museum. The neighborhood has completely changed since the night of my father's burial.

I glance toward the site where I stood the night they buried my father. The ground is now covered with sparse grass. The stones are gone.

"Uncle Will," I ask, "where is my father's grave?"

He looks at me, his eyes distant and distracted. But before he can answer, the latch on the oak door turns with a loud metallic snap.

Mr. Jesup walks in. I stand at attention and extend my right hand. "Delighted to see you, sir," I say, pronouncing my words carefully. "Perhaps you can tell me where my father's grave is?"

"For goodness' sake — English! Wallace, I see you haven't wasted the museum's money in bringing up this young man!" Mr. Jesup does not shake my hand but instead kneels to my level, cupping the back of my neck with his thick palm. "Well, Mene, it is a pleasure to see how you have matured since you were at my house. A fine New York gentleman! I look forward to speaking more with you — but for now, if you'll excuse us . . ."

77

He escorts me into his small outer room, then returns to the office and shuts the door behind him.

They have moved him, I tell myself. The museum has expanded and another wing is being built, so the grave has been moved to another place. In Greenland we moved graves when the summer sea flooded the gravesite.

Mr. Jesup's secretary is not here today, so I sit at her mahogany desk. The chair is covered with a thick cushion, and because it has conformed to her generous shape I feel as if I am straddling a hilltop.

I play with the telephone. I draw animals on her stenography pad. When I become tired of that I climb on the desk, then jump onto the Oriental rug, falling into a somersault. In doing so I nearly knock over an empty drinking glass, but I catch it before it hits the rug.

That's when I hear the raised voices through the door.

I sidle closer. The walls are thick, and it is difficult to make out words. Mr. Jesup sounds bewildered and angry, Uncle Will clipped and defensive.

My hands are sweating on the glass. It squeaks against my fingers as I return it to the desk.

Sound and glass. A memory comes to me.

Holding the open end of the glass to the wall, I place my ear on the closed end and listen.

Some of the language is complex, and I don't understand it all. But I have developed a good memory for the sound of words, which I can look up later. In later years I will be able to reconstruct this conversation — and although it is not exact, I am certain of the gist:

". . . a notice in *The New York Times,* Wallace," says Mr. Jesup. "The *Times!* It is embarrassing to the museum to see your debts displayed in public."

"It is a personal matter, sir," Uncle Will replies, "owing to problems with my dairy. I assure you I am paying it back."

"I trust you, Wallace. When you tell me your problems are personal, I respect that." Papers shuffle and Mr. Jesup lights a cigar. I can smell it. "But let us talk about the bone-bleaching house. It is on your property, but it belongs to us."

"The macerating plant has nothing to do with my dairy, sir. My workers are paid by the city, for work done on museum specimens."

"And our contractor, Chesley, has billed for three months of work done there — Chesley, who builds *museum cases.*"

"Chesley is an excellent all-around carpenter."

"Indeed. Tell me, Wallace, the city pays for all construction work on the museum — including at your plant — is that correct?"

"Of course, sir."

"The contractors bill us. We pass the bill to the city. The city then pays the contractors directly."

"Yes, sir."

"And you happen to be the man in the middle. The museum's man. You take the bill from the contractor; then you send it on to the city for payment."

"It is my job as superintendent."

"Quite a lot of power you have, Wallace."

"Power, sir?"

Mr. Jesup is silent for a long time. "These men have families. They need the city to pay them quickly. They need you to hurry the bill along. If you don't — if you happen to lose their bill, or if it sits on your desk forgotten — they could face dire financial trouble."

"That would be true, but what are you implying, sir?"

"A crooked man would abuse that power. A crooked man might delay those bills. Make the contractors sweat. When they complain, he might make a deal in order to speed the bills along. He would simply ask the contractors to bill for a larger sum — say, double. Then, when the contractors received that great sum, they would keep only the amount that represented their work. The rest — that extra hundred percent — would go to this crooked man. As a payment for speeding up the process. We call this *extortion*, Mr. Wallace. It is the province of certain moneylenders and politicians — *crooked* men, not employees of the New York Museum of Natural History. Not you. I have always placed full trust in you."

"And I have always treasured that trust."

"Yes. Well, I called you here to say that my colleagues have asked me to conduct an investigation into these bills. I plan to do so, but I expect to find that everything has been honest and aboveboard, and that my trust for you shall remain unshaken."

"Thank you, Mr. Jesup."

The chairs scrape back. I race to the desk and replace the drinking glass.

Uncle Will emerges, still clutching his hat. His eyes are far away.

"Look!" I say, holding up one of my stenography-pad drawings.

He keeps walking to the door. "Let us go home now, Minik."

The Fantods

"You are having *what*, Minik?" Willie asks.

"Fantods." I swing my baseball bat lazily from one side to the other as we approach the high school field. "It means jitters, nervousness. I looked it up. I am having fantods about everything."

"Like what?"

"Well, playing the Spuyten Duyvils, for one thing."

"We can lick them."

"Easy for you to say. You're seventeen."

"Fourteen is perfect for baseball. You have a smaller strike zone. Is that all you're worried about?"

"Well . . . no. I think about Aunt Rhetta's health a lot. And Uncle Will's job."

Willie puts his arm around my shoulder. "*I* see the glass half full, Minik. It's all for the best that Pop lost his job. Now he can stay home to take care of Mom, see? Now, buck up. We're going to smash these flatfoots."

"Flat *feet*."

"Pardon me, professor."

The Duyvils are on the field now, hitting fungoes. Very, very hard and high fungoes. As the runners practice sliding, their spikes glint like knives in the sun, and I am acutely aware that having survived a life of sickness and great personal tragedy, I have chosen to place my life in the hands of a six-foot fastball pitcher named Gorilla.

A girl is waiting by the backstop, watching through the fence, and Willie taps her on the shoulder. "This is my brother, Minik," he says. "The best baseball player east of the Hudson. Minik, this is Matilda."

I have just added another to my growing collection of fantods. "Hell," I say with a catch in my throat, quickly adding, "o."

Matilda makes a slight curtsy. Then, very carefully, with an impish glint in her eye, she says, *"Hi-nay-nuck-who-nay."* It means, *Hello, how are you?*

Her pronunciation is dreadful. Her voice, however, is intoxicating.

"I taught her to say that," says Willie, beaming with pride.

Matilda is shorter than me, under five feet tall. Her hair is the color of the Arctic night, and her eyes would thaw the ice cap from Smith Sound to the North Pole.

"Aihugia," I reply. *I am fine.*

My lively Eskimo imagination sees many possibilities with Matilda. All of them make my face flush, so to compensate I conjure up sober thoughts of school — equations, textbooks, Charles Darwin (*survival of the fittest, strutting, plumage, displays of virility*), Isaac Newton (*two bodies exerting an equal and opposite attraction on each other*). None of this helps.

"HEY, IGLOO BOY, YOU IN OR OUT?" yells Sluggo Barnes of Pelham Bay, who plays for the Duyvils.

"I must play now," I say, in a voice that dips and jumps unexpectedly like a foot breaking through thin ice.

I am in a fog. On the first pitch the bat slips out of my hands and flies to first base. "You need to wipe the whale blubber off your fingers?" taunts Sluggo.

"He's in love," mumbles our catcher, Pete Schermerhorn.

"With what?" says Bud Bernsen, our center fielder. "A polar bear?"

"There are no polar bears in the Arctic, you halfwit," snaps Pete.

"That's the *Antarctic,* pea brain," says Bud. "No polar bears in the Antarctic, no penguins in the Arctic."

Gorilla throws a high hard one that makes me dive for my life. But the next pitch is fat and down the middle, and I somehow hit it back so hard that it nearly decapitates Gorilla. Running full tilt, I beat the throw to first base by a mile.

But as I am about to stomp on the base, a leg darts out in front of me. My feet leave the ground. My neck snaps back so fast that I lose consciousness.

Suddenly I am on my back and staring into the face of Gorilla. "You did that on purpose!" he says.

"Pick on someone your own size!" Bud shouts, shoving Gorilla aside. "Or at your own intelligence — if you can find someone that stupid."

84

Now Gorilla's teammates and mine are shoving and shouting, piling on top of one another with arms and legs flailing. I stagger to my feet and look for Matilda on the sidelines.

Instead I see Uncle Will, running toward us.

The pile breaks up. At the bottom Gorilla sheepishly rolls off Willie, whose mouth is bleeding and whose body is covered with mud.

Uncle Will grabs his son by the arm. "Come quickly. You, too, Minik."

We run off the field and climb onto Uncle Will's run-down carriage. He explains that Aunt Rhetta is sick and that Willie and I must stay with her until he can locate the doctor. "Nothing serious, but Lizzie is off today and I don't want to leave Mother alone." He gives Willie an admonishing sidelong glance. "And please, before she sees you, wash the blood off your face and change your clothes."

At the house we jump off and run inside. Willie calls for his mother, but there is no answer. In the master bedroom, we stand at the doorjamb. A coal stove is crackling with heat. Aunt Rhetta is lying on her bed beneath several blankets, eyes closed.

"Auntie Rhetta!" I call out, running into the room, but Willie pulls me back, reminding me that she needs rest.

Aunt Rhetta's eyes flutter open. "It appears that you have been playing the Spuyten Duyvils," she says.

"Oh, rot!" Willie runs out, and soon I hear splashing from the washroom.

"Can I get you something, Auntie?" I ask.

She smiles. "Dear, thoughtful, brave Minik. A wash would not hurt you, either."

I do not return to school for the next few weeks. Instead I stay home, helping prepare food and run errands. I answer Aunt Rhetta's letters and plan menus. This aggravates Uncle Will and my teachers, but I explain that I care far more for Aunt Rhetta than I do for Messrs. Darwin and Newton. Lizzie huffs and puffs and says she'll "decay with idleness" because of all the work I'm doing.

Aunt Rhetta understands. She enjoys having my company. Often she asks for Eskimo legends and songs. I remember only a few. My memories of Greenland have faded so. I have begun to think, to dream, in English. I try to remember, to hold on. My heart is still that of a Smith Sound Eskimo, and there I live with the comfort of snow, the excitement of the hunt, and the extremeness of light and dark. But my brain is, I'm afraid to say, a New Yorker's. And I feel my soul, like the winter sun, slipping, slipping, below the horizon.

In late April a winter storm rages outside the house. The blowing snow sounds like pebbles thrown against the window. Aunt Rhetta is wheezing and miserable as I bring her a cup of tea. "Tell me about the stars, Minik," she says.

I pull up the Windsor chair and try to remember the words.

"When people die they rise to the sky," I begin.
"They live in villages, waiting for the ones they love.
At night you can see them:
Their igloos are brightly lit.
The stars are windows.
And inside them, if you look closely,
You see their faces,
Smiling."

When I finish, the ticking of the clock is the only sound
I hear. Nothing has changed in the room, and yet somehow
I know everything is different. I place the covers over her,
kiss her cheek, and sit by her side. I think of my mother —
Anaana — and despite my New Yorker brain, I start to cry.
Why? *Why is it happening again?*

When Uncle Will arrives home, he listens to her heartbeat and immediately carries her out to the carriage. She has
become frail and he holds her as if she is a child.

I follow him to the door. Willie has come home with his
father, and the two of us watch, weeping, as the carriage
vanishes into the snow.

Windows in the Sky

"I think I see him sometimes."

I can hardly believe I am admitting this. But I can say things to Matilda that I have never been able to say to anyone else.

We are sitting on a bench on Uncle Will's porch, hours after Aunt Rhetta's funeral. The breeze carries the sweet scent of viburnum, the first flower of spring, Aunt Rhetta's favorite. Inside, several families have gathered for tea and conversation.

Her passing has hit me hard. It is 1904, six years since anyone close to me has died. I have told Matilda all about my father's burial, about the way Aunt Rhetta held me and comforted me afterward, while I cried for days and days.

And now I have just divulged my deepest secret.

"You see your father — you mean, in a dream?" Matilda asks.

"The Eskimos know that the dead come back to visit," I explain. "A spirit of a dead person can be kind and helpful and loving — but if his body hasn't been buried properly, he will be angry and haunt you always."

"That's creepy!" Matilda says, moving closer to me. "When you see your father, is he happy or angry?"

"I can't tell. He should be angry, I think. We have lots of taboos about death and burial, which must be followed or terrible things will happen. The museum broke lots of those. I don't even know where they put his body. It's missing from the place where they buried him."

"They probably moved it to a proper cemetery," Matilda says.

"I thought I saw him today, at Aunt Rhetta's burial. Nearly hidden among the crowd, so I couldn't make out his face. That's the way it is — I see him for a moment, or just a part of him among other people. Sometimes I hear his voice. On the night he was buried, he cried out to me."

I feel her eyes on the side of my face. I have said too much. "Well, at least that's what I think," I say. "It seems real."

"Maybe it is," she says. "Maybe you *are* seeing him, the way people see God, or Jesus."

No, I want to say, that's not exactly it. In Matilda's world, God is the Holy Spirit, love and forgiveness, trust and salvation, judgment and wrath, good and evil. Seeing God is a respectable thing. But seeing dead people is crazy. Dead is dead. Dead is carbon and nitrogen and calcium. Man is not a spirit but a system — evolution and respiration, biology and chemistry, history and anthropology.

This is the thing I cannot yet tell Matilda: that where I come from what is seen and measured is no different from what is unseen and felt.

"Do you believe in God?" I ask.

"Yes. And I believe that people live on after they die, in heaven."

Above us, the North Star has pierced the twilight sky. "Do you know what *we* believe? That the stars are windows into igloos where the dead live."

Matilda laughs. "Now *that's* silly."

Silly? This hurts, but I know she cannot understand. *Each to his own magic,* my father said.

We watch quietly as the sky turns dark. Matilda leans back and points upward. "Look! There's old Abraham Lincoln . . . and poor President McKinley. . . ."

A sharp wind rustles the trees and sweeps through the porch. Although the air has become quite cold, it feels as if a pair of soft arms has come gently from behind me, wrapping me with their warmth. "Hello, Aunt Rhetta," I say.

"I see her too," Matilda says.

I feel a soft kiss on my cheek. Matilda lays her head on my shoulder, and we stay that way as stars flood the night sky.

Discovery

"Mr. Wallace? Mr. Minik Wallace? Will you please come back to Earth?"

Mrs. Rutherford slaps her yardstick on the desk. The other students snicker as I snap to attention. It has been two weeks since Aunt Rhetta has died. I am back at school, in person if not in spirit. Catching up on my studies has been impossible. Not that it was ever easy. I want to learn. I want to see my teachers smile with surprise. Some of them cannot believe such a "savage" can actually read, let alone reason. But although I perform well, school bores me. Sitting at a desk, confined by tight clothing, I want to scream! I want to leave the building and never come back.

Since returning to school after Aunt Rhetta's death, I have not been myself. I have felt sad and angry, snapping at friends and teachers — even Willie. Most of the students have been understanding; they, too, knew and loved Aunt Rhetta.

As Mrs. Rutherford writes math problems on the board, my attention wanders to the window again. The fog has settled so thickly that the sky and earth are the same, a two-dimensional flatness that somehow hints of limitless depth. It is an eerie morning, and I assume that is why everyone seems to be acting strange today. They fall quiet and avert their eyes whenever I enter a room.

At lunch I see Pete and Bud at a table, talking animatedly with a group of girls. I do not care for these girls. They are, in my opinion, the opposite of Matilda — brassy, loud, and ignorant. I will explode if I have to answer one more question such as "Do you really ride on polar bears?" or "Is it true Eskimos eat their babies?"

Pete is holding a newspaper article, reading aloud. I hear my name, which surprises me. It has been years since the newspapers ran articles about "little Mene."

When Pete sees me approach, he stops abruptly, shoving the clipping into his shirt pocket.

The girls are silent as I sit. "San Francisco built back up?" I ask.

Blank faces.

"From the fire," I continue. "Well, then, how about the stock market? Is everyone poor yet? I thought Pete was reading you the news. Or was he just describing the fashions?"

One of the girls, Philomena, scowls at me. "We *do* know how to read," she says, "little mini-Mene."

I take a bite of my roast potatoes. "Well, congratulations. There *has* been some progress since I've been here."

"Who are you to insult us?" mutters a blond girl named Liesl.

"It was a compliment," I reply.

"Someone left his manners at the igloo," says another girl, Rebecca. "His common sense, too."

"Girls . . ." Pete says with a warning tone.

But I am on a short fuse. "I could scoop up the common sense at this table with a teaspoon," I say calmly.

"Maybe you can use it," says Philomena. "Your family didn't seem to have much of it when you were snookered away to the nasty city."

My fist tightens around my fork. "You wouldn't survive a week in my village. You wouldn't know a polar bear from a snowman."

"Oh, really? Well, at least I wouldn't mistake a *tree* for my father!"

Pete springs out of his chair. "Phil, you're over the line!"

"A *what*?" I say, but Pete grabs my arm and leads me away from the table. The other girls look shocked.

"Ignore her," Pete says as we stumble toward the exit.

"A tree?" I ask.

"It's nothing. You know how the newspapers work."

"No, Pete. Tell me."

He takes me out the cafeteria door, muttering to the teacher in charge that I have to go to the school nurse. We turn a corner and find ourselves alone in the corridor.

"You can't believe everything you read," Pete says. "That's what I was trying to tell them."

"The article was about me, wasn't it?" I ask.

Pete is sweating. He looks as if he is about to cry. "I can't show it to you, Minik."

I try to pull it from his pocket, but he lurches back. "I will fight you for it, right here," I say. "And you will lose."

"You don't want to try that." Pete has at least eight inches and fifty pounds on me.

93

I rear back and slug him in the face. As he stumbles, his eyes wide with surprise, I throw a block at his midsection.

Pete falls to the floor and I jump on him. I see the article in his shirt pocket and pull it out.

"Minik, don't!" he says, grabbing my wrist.

I jump away. By the light of the window I unfold the article.

> . . . The hospital and the museum briefly disputed the disposition of the corpse of the dead Eskimo, Kooshoo, and it was agreed finally that students at Bellevue should make use of it in the dissecting-room, and afterward the skeleton should be preserved and mounted in the Museum of Natural History. . . .

Kooshoo. That was what they called my father.

Disposition of the corpse?

I start to read on, numbed, but suddenly the article is gone — snatched out of my hand by Pete. His face is red, his eyes moist.

"That's a lie," I say. "They buried him. I was there. I saw it."

Pete shakes his head. "They fooled you, Minik. That wasn't your father. They had already done . . . those things."

"The dissecting room, the skeleton?"

"Yes."

"Give me the article!"

Pete steps back. "You don't want to read the rest."

"Who did they bury, then? *Who was that?*"

"Not *who*," Pete says softly. "*What*."

I listen to his explanation, but it does not register at first. It makes the corridor seem to spin and the light spill from the fixtures. It makes my world turn upside down.

My father was a log.

Ownership

"You *knew*," I shout at Uncle Will. "You had to know! You stood there while they made a mockery of my father! While they buried a stick. *How could you do that?*"

It was simple. With all the construction in the city, all the toppled trees, a four-and-a-half-foot wooden log was easy to find.

They knew that the Eskimos covered their dead, wrapped them in bulky skins. It didn't matter what you put between the skins — as long as it was the same size and had a little heft, it could pass as a body.

After all, they only had to fool a child.

Uncle Will seems to sag so deeply that he becomes part of the chair fabric. His face, which has settled into old age since Aunt Rhetta's death, is drained of color. His eyes are fixed on mine.

"It wasn't my idea, Minik," he says. "But they had already taken your father's body, and you were so upset. If we hadn't had a burial —"

"*You let them take him!*" I reply. "For science. For study. To chop him up and poke at his organs. What did the students see? Did they see how big his heart was? Did they feel the strength in his arms? Did his smile make them understand that the world was good and safe? Is that what science taught them?"

Uncle Will gestures for me to sit, but I stay standing. "I was the superintendent," he says softly. "I had no say over matters of science. They had their own ideas about ownership."

"*Ownership*? How can Boas own a person?"

"Boas had a mission. His colleagues believed that Eskimos — and Indians, and other so-called aboriginal people — were arrested on the evolutionary chain, that they were somehow less intelligent, less developed. He was determined to prove those anthropologists wrong. He wanted to study everything about Eskimos — biology, language, culture, anatomy. He believed that this kind of understanding would lead to an appreciation of the beauty of your people — and ultimately preserve you."

"Eskimos have been in Greenland for thousands of years without Mr. Boas trying to preserve us! Tell me, Uncle Will, did he do the same to Atangana's body — and Nuktaq's and Aviaq's?"

Uncle Will nods silently.

"And what about the barrels on the *Hope*? Did you know about them? Full of bones and skulls. I have never forgotten them. They were Eskimos, too, weren't they?"

"Yes. Peary brought them back from Greenland. He took them from their graves. I suppose he didn't think anyone would notice."

"Of course not. They were cargo, just like Ahnighito.

He stole them, Uncle Will. Or did he think it was a trade? He gives us knives and guns, and he takes whatever he wants — sacred stones, live people, dead people. Or maybe this was part of a bigger plan — he knew we would all die, so the museum could have fresh new skeletons to study. Are they waiting for me, too? Are you going to collect the money when you deliver Skeleton Number Five? Too bad you're not working there anymore. You could bill the city for twice the amount!"

"Please, Minik." Uncle Will reaches for my hand, but I pull it away. "None of that is true. They didn't know your people would die. For all their science, they just didn't know. When we realized you wouldn't handle the climate here, we thought it best to get you out of the city. I had the space for you to live, and Rhetta and I wanted you to feel at home."

"You took us because the museum was paying you."

"Money had nothing to do with it. They welshed on most of it, anyway. And once I was fired, they cut me off completely."

I stare at a photograph on Uncle Will's desk. It shows me in knickers and a cap, my long hair touching my shoulder, posing with a bicycle on the day I received it as a gift from Willie. I remember being happy that day, but my face looks strangely glum. "In my village," I say, "if you were an orphan, you most likely died. During a good hunting season, a kind family would throw you a scrap or two. But if the hunting was bad, you would be tossed out to the cold. An orphan was a burden on the survival of the group."

"That's . . . inhumane," Uncle Will says.

"Not if the village doesn't have enough to go around. Feeding one more person, spreading the food supply too thin, could mean death for everyone." I look him in the eye. "Why did you do it, Uncle Will? Why did you educate and feed me when you had no money?"

"Because I love you."

My chest starts to heave, and I have a great urge to leap into Uncle Will's lap the way I did when I was younger. The truth is, I love him, too.

"When the museum collects bones," I begin, "how does it get them from the bodies? Is it like skinning a seal?"

Uncle Will blanches. "Not exactly. Here it is often done by machine. A chemical process. The body is . . . macerated."

"Like the plant on your farm, in Lawyersville."

Uncle Will looks away. As he nods, I see him blinking as if something is in his eye.

"You used that for animals," I say, "so the museum could mount skeletons."

"Yes," Uncle Will replies.

"You were going to use it on Hilda, the elephant — but you didn't, because you knew how much I cared for her."

"Yes."

It takes me a moment to form the next question. "Did you ever use it for anything else?"

"Anything else?"

"Besides animals, I mean. Any other kind of body."

Uncle Will does not reply. But his expression tells me everything.

I rise from my chair. And I begin to run.

Hikup Hinaa

I run through streets of black blood as the trees shake with laughter and the houses with arms folded cluck, *How could you have been so stupid?* My senses disconnect and reconnect willy-nilly in my brain; the cold shrieks, the colors stink of decay, and my feet pound flashes of light. Carriage drivers shout obscenities as I careen into their paths, letting my legs choose the direction my mind cannot. And I arrive, in the end, at the only safe place for me: Matilda's house.

Out of breath I sit on her lawn, my back against the basement wall as my thoughts cohere like vapor into droplets of dew.

I must think.

I must talk to her. I must tell her what happened. No one else will understand. Not even my best friend, my brother. He is one of them. He knew. He must have known.

Through the branches of a dying chrysanthemum bush I can see the sidewalk. Soon, I know, she will be returning from school.

In a few moments or perhaps an hour, I hear her laughter, light and flutelike on the breeze. I wait, gathering my strength, until she comes into view.

She is not alone.

Willie has her arm. He whispers something to her, and she tilts her head, resting it on his shoulder.

They are both smiling.

My life, my reality, has come to *hikup hinaa*, the edge of the ice. And the ice has broken.

"Minik?" I hear Matilda say. "Is that you?"

But I am gone. I am flying across the lawn, leaping over a hedge, taking to the streets again, away.

I reach the High Bridge and clamber down the rock scree just north of its base, by the water. A schooner heads through the narrow arch, its sails slack.

I stuff my pockets full of rocks and take off my shoes. The channel is deep here. I will sink to the bottom instantly.

From above I hear the puttering of motorcars and the giggling of lovers. And then a voice.

"*Inovaglutik nunanuaminut uterpaglik!*"

It is an old saying. "May the living return to the land they hold dear."

I look up. My father is dancing on the railing of the bridge. But he is a skeleton, nothing but bones over clothing, his skull capped with black hair. Somehow, even though he has no face, I can see his smile.

"*Inussuarana?*" I call out. Are you man or spirit?

But he just laughs and dances, weightless and oblivious to danger, his spindly bones clacking like auks' wings. Slowly the flesh forms over his body, his parka plumps out, and there he is — my *ataata*, healthy looking as he was in life!

He catches my eye, smiles, and then moves both arms in

a signaling motion, pointing toward the Bronx. *"Attuk!"* To the right!

I look in that direction.

Three blue uniforms converge on me. Someone grabs my ankle, another my arm. I am surrounded by policemen.

"You scared us there, sonny boy," says a voice.

"Smell his breath," says another.

I am craning my neck, looking back to where my father was, but all I see is a man walking a dog.

And I scream his name, calling him back, back to rescue me, as the men carry me away.

Part Three
Quebec, May 7, 1909

Attuk

"*Ataata!*"

My own cry jolts me out of the dream.

The arches of the High Bridge, the scrubby sloped banks, vanish like blown snow in the night. I am in a strange bedroom, five years later, pitch-dark but for the faint reflected flicker of a distant lamplight.

Through the wall comes the smell of baking bread, the sound of chairs scraping on a wooden floor. It is the café next door to the *pension* in Quebec City, and I am in a first-floor room, sharing a wall with it. Someone has moved me while I was asleep.

At this point, frankly, I'm surprised to be here still. Madame Jolliet surely must have wanted to throw me out. I am no doubt in debt to the priest for his persuasive powers.

I sit up. Outside I see the light of the unrisen sun already bruising the horizon. My fever has broken and I feel well rested for the first time in days.

Outside a light moves along the river. A supply ship.

The Eskimos know that the dead come back.

Matilda was the only one who took me seriously. My

father was there, outside the *pension,* along the river. He was on top of the High Bridge.

Each time, he was trying to tell me something.

Was he angry, because of what happened to him at the museum? Was he asking me to join him in a happy place or luring me to death?

I don't remember the lore — the rules of death, the penalties for broken taboos. It has been too long.

Both times I saw my father, he signaled to me. That is what I remember most. The first time, years ago, he was gesturing toward the Bronx. The second time, yesterday, he signaled twice, both times up the Côte de la Montagne.

Were they warnings, instructions to make sure I joined him in the afterworld — *drown yourself quickly; the police are coming! Be careful of the people on the sidewalk! Jump now or the men in the café will catch you!* — or were they something else?

The movements were broad, strong. *Attuk,* he said both times. To the right.

And suddenly, like the world outside forming out of darkness, I see what he meant.

Not to the right.

To the east.

How could I be so stupid? My father was not telling me to join him. *He was telling me what to do.*

He wanted me to keep going. To do what I came here for.

To continue to Newfoundland and find a ship to Greenland.

Home.

My father wants me home.

I stand. My legs are not too shaky. The rest has done me some good. It will have to be good enough.

I notice a pad of paper on the dresser. The priest has left a note: *Dear Minik, I will see you for breakfast. Madame Jolliet has graciously agreed to these new lodgings while the door upstairs is being repaired. I have taken the liberty of supplementing your wardrobe with some store-bought garments — and something from my church's charity collection. It is hanging by the door.*

On a rack to my right hangs a beautiful woolen overcoat. I feel a pang of guilt as I put it on. It is a perfect fit, and I will not be able to repay the priest or even thank him in person.

Pulling out the drawers, I find a new shirt and clean underwear neatly folded among my meager belongings. Quickly I stuff them all into the valise, alongside my now dog-eared photo of my father.

The sun has broken the horizon. I must leave soon. Quickly I take a sheet from the pad of paper and write the priest a short note.

I cannot possibly thank you enough for your kindnesses. I can also never hope to fully explain what drove me to my rash act yesterday. You will read someday, if you have not already, of the way my father's body was treated after his death — that the New York Museum of Natural History keeps his bones in a drawer ("for study"!) and refuses to give them back to me for a burial.

I will remember you as I do my Uncle Will and Dob —
William Wallace and Chester Beecroft — the only people who
truly cared for me.

You see, I attempted to kill myself once before, but the
police caught me and gave me back to Uncle Will. I stayed with
him for four more years, until his money ran out and he was
forced into menial jobs and smaller apartments — until he
could no longer afford to educate me and had to send his own
son to live with relatives. While I worked a job — "temporarily" —
his old friend Dob took an interest, going all the way to the
White House to insist that Peary pay for my schooling.

None of it worked.

I cannot burden them (and you) any further. It is time to
return home. I will attempt to find passage on a ship from
Newfoundland to Greenland. I have missed one already, I
know, but there is bound to be another. To make the money, I
will work, beg, or steal. Please destroy this note and do not
attempt to stop me.

In the meantime, my love and thanks.

Pray for me.

Mene Peary Wallace
(Original signature of declarant.)

P.S. Before I left New York, I gave an interview to a
reporter for the San Francisco Examiner (Dob's idea). If you
can get a copy, it will tell you all, in much greater detail.

I seal the envelope. It is late. I must go.
Quietly I leave the room, not latching the door for fear

of waking Madame Jolliet. I hold my breath to avoid coughing out my congested lungs.

I turn left on Côte de la Montagne and head up the hill. It winds around to a steep, rickety staircase that leads to the Haute-Ville, the Upper Town. A thin, balding man is about to climb it. I say the word "train" and imitate a chugging engine — and he points me, blessedly, to a location in the Lower Town. "Rue de la Gare-du-Palais," he says.

As I follow the Old Port around the confluence of the Saint Lawrence and Saint Charles rivers, the train station looms like a turreted brick palace. I am surprised by the number of travelers at this hour.

I head for the tracks and look in the shadows. There, squatting by an upended barrel, is a coal-faced bindle stiff. A hobo.

"Brigus," I say. "Newfoundland."

"*Ah, oui.*" He gestures vaguely toward one of the trains on the sidings, then pats the ground next to him by way of invitation.

I sit. "Minik," I say, pointing to myself.

"Jean-Claude." He pulls a cigarette from his coat pocket, which I eagerly accept. But once I take a puff I begin to cough violently. He hands me a flask and I take a swig.

The liquid is foul. I gag, spewing out the liquid in a spasm of coughing that I'm afraid will turn me inside out.

This gives Jean-Claude a fit of giggles, and he pulls a black oblong object from his pocket. "*Banane?*"

"*Oui!*"

I peel the nearly liquefied fruit and eat it slowly, letting it soothe my throat. Before I know it, my head is resting on Jean-Claude's shoulder and I am drifting off to sleep.

The wetness on my shoulder wakens me.

It seeps up from the rocky ground, where I am lying, in a puddle. I try to open my eyes, but I am facing east, and the morning sun beats down at me through a clear sky.

A train whistle blasts, carried on a stiff breeze. The cold penetrates to my skin, and I realize my new coat is gone. I try to sit up, but my head is pounding. I feel a hard bump above my right ear.

Along with my coat, Jean-Claude has disappeared. So has my valise, with the photograph of my father inside.

I struggle to stand, but the pain in my head is like relentless hammer blows. Holding to the side of the station, I emerge into the plaza in front of the station.

The sun now blazes in the eastern sky. Uniformed footmen assist people climbing out of carriages, which line the Rue de la Gare-du-Palais in both directions. The passengers, mostly men in hats and wool coats, walk purposefully toward the station entrance, ignoring the various hawkers that line the way.

One of the hawkers, gaunt and hunched, is holding out a coat, shouting a price. It is Jean-Claude.

If I approach across the plaza he will see me, so I retreat to the shadows and make my way around the station. Emerging from the other side, I approach him silently from behind.

The hurried travelers, who do not lack for fine outer-wear, are ignoring his entreaties. In his left hand he holds out the valise, which had been hidden under the draped coat.

I grab the handle. Jean-Claude spins around, holding tight. He is scrappy and strong. "Gendarme!" he cries out.

I leap up and spit, catching him in the right eye.

I pull hard at both jacket and valise, but he clings tight, grimacing, stumbling. We both collapse to the ground.

The coat falls across his face. I straddle his body, keeping his arms pinned to his sides. With one hand I feel for his neck through the coat's fabric and grab tight, keeping his head still. With the other hand, I press hard over his nose and mouth, smothering him until his muffled, gagging screams become soundless and his grip loosens.

Then I take the coat and valise and run.

A crowd has formed around us, but they jump aside. I hear shrill whistles, and from all corners of the plaza blue uniforms converge on me. I reverse direction, heading west, back into the crowd, into the confused and fearful travelers. Some of the men try to reach for me, but I am too fast. I emerge from the other side.

There Jean-Claude waits, legs planted, holding a knife.

I stop short. Behind me the whistles and frantic foot-steps are coming nearer. I turn to look over my shoulder.

And all goes black.

A Man

He is carrying me across the plaza. Around us no one moves. The police, the travelers and porters and carriage drivers, they stand aside stiff as ice hummocks.

His footsteps are light and even, and I feel as if I am riding on a sled over new-fallen snow. The congestion of the city surrounds us, but the wind is all I hear. The wind and his voice, singing to me.

"Inovaglutik nunanuaminut uterpaglik . . ."

Curled in his arms, wrapped in a warm anorak, I see only the sun's blinding glare off the river.

I remember our old game. Squinting at the Central Park lake to convince ourselves we were home. I have the urge to play that game now, but I cannot. I no longer know what home is. All I do know is that I have made a mistake. That coming here to Quebec City was not the right thing to do. That back at the *pension* I had read my father's signal all wrong.

I apologize.

He finishes a verse, then pauses. His footsteps are silent.

"Inussuarana?" he finally asks. Are you man or spirit?

It is a strange question for him to be asking me.

"*Inussuanga*," I reply. I am a man.

I cannot see his face. But I know he is smiling.

He continues to sing. And I, soothed and secure, fall asleep.

The Church of Peary

"He's coming to?"

"Poor little thing."

"He's been very sick."

"Please, open the window. The vapors, you know. They gather. He must have air."

I must be dreaming, because I hear Dob's voice along with the priest's. And someone else. A woman.

"Minik? Minik, how are you feeling?"

I force my eyes open and turn onto my back.

The face that peers back at me is not my father's but the priest's. Through the haze of fading half-dreams I see a ceiling fan turning lazily. Behind me voices filter through the walls of my room in the *pension*.

"How are you feeling, Minik?" the priest asks.

Dob is now by his side. "'Morning, chum," he says. "I'll bet you're hungry. And I'll bet you didn't expect me for breakfast!"

Dob? Morning?

I look out the window at the bustle of workers. The yeasty smell of baking bread filters into the room and I realize Dob is right. It is morning and I *am* hungry.

"Am I dreaming?" I ask.

Dob laughs. He is robust, with a broad nose, a ready smile, and sharp eyes that leap and dance. "I'd say seeing my face would qualify as a nightmare."

"How did I get here?"

"You have been here for days," the priest replies.

He does not know that I've been to the train station. I must have been delivered back here before he found out. But who delivered me?

I remember the arms, the voice — my father's.

It's like seeing God.

No. There is still an early-morning sky outside. I could not have made it there and back so quickly.

I sink back to the pillow. "It *was* a dream. . . ."

"Can't anyone see he needs some support for his head?" I turn to see a tall woman whose wavy blond hair is swept up into a hive, with one lock hanging loose in the back. She moves with an animated grace across the room, taking a pillow from the small sofa and bringing it to me.

"Men," she says, propping it behind my head. "Absolutely hopeless."

Her eyes are dark and enormous. The men defer to her. Their behavior — in fact, the climate of the room itself — seems dependent on her smile.

Dob clears his throat. "Minik, this is Miss Vesta Tilley," he says with an air of great expectancy.

"My valise — my coat — where are they?" I ask.

"In your dresser drawer, safe and sound," the priest says. "And hanging on the rack."

"Ah . . . you know, Minik, the *actress?*" Dob continues, glancing from me to the woman uncomfortably. "*Vesta Tilley?* The toast of Longacre Square?"

"*Times* Square is what it's called now, Chester," Miss Tilley corrects him.

I know Miss Tilley's name. Most New Yorkers do. Her ramrod-straight back, dark arresting eyes, and broad shoulders have earned her fame as the most skilled female performer of male roles — putting many lesser men to shame.

"Pleased to meet you," I say.

"Charmed." Miss Tilley seems considerably less in awe of herself than Dob is. "Your friend Mr. Beecroft told me all about your plight, my dear, which I found an inexcusable outrage. Not your actions, of course, however misguided they may be — they are entirely understandable given the way you have been treated all your life — but the fact that that dreadful husk of a man, Peary, will not give you safe passage to your ancestral home. As I told Mr. Beecroft, 'If it is merely the means you require in order to retrieve the child, I am nothing if not a woman of both ways *and* means, and in fact I plan personally to escort you to his door' — and, well, here we are. May I get you something to drink?"

I feel compelled to applaud but restrain myself. "Yes, please," I say.

Miss Tilley walks out the door, into the street, and around to the café. I can hear her shouts of "*Garçon! Vite! Vite!*" through the wall.

"When Mr. Green alerted me to the newspaper coverage of your case," the priest explains, "and I read about your

116

letter to Mr. Beecroft last afternoon, I made it my task to contact him by the telephone. He was grateful for news of your whereabouts and left within hours."

"Thanks to the remarkable Miss Tilley," says Dob. "We traveled all night by train, and she remained quite awake."

"Mr. Wallace, I might add, has been contacted, too," the priest says. "He was utterly relieved to know you were alive, and he was grateful for our intervention."

"Your Uncle Will had a notion you may be trying to reach Ottawa, to board Commander Radford's ship," Dob goes on. "But that would have taken you to the northern lands of Canada, hardly close to your home."

"I wanted Captain Bartlett's relief ship for Dr. Cook," I say. "But I did not move fast enough. That voyage has left already. I thought I might try my luck in Brigus — a whaler, perhaps."

"Oh, good heavens, my boy, any whaler from New-foundland would not take you *near* Smith Sound. You would have ended up a thousand miles from your home with no family or means of travel!" Dob pounds his fist on the dresser. "Confound it, Minik, the old boys in Peary's little Arctic Club, the scientists at the museum — their treatment of you has not been barbaric; it's been inhuman. Little wonder you've been driven to this. I was hoping you'd stay in the States and go to college. If you want you to go home, so be it — but you must do it in the right way!"

"And what is that, Dob?"

Miss Tilley barges cheerfully through the door, carrying a tray with a steaming basket of pastries and jam, a pot of coffee, and four stacked cups. "A hearty meal for all!" she says, quickly setting up a breakfast area on the dresser.

Dob hands me a croissant and takes one for himself. "Now, Miss Tilley and I discussed this matter on the way here, and as we see it, the responsibility for you lies wholly in the hands of Mr. Peary."

"As you no doubt know, Peary has created for himself a certain . . . theatrical aura," adds Miss Tilley. "The national hero. America's own Robert Falcon Scott. Of course, no one here actually *sees* what he does in the Arctic — very convenient for him, of course. Nevertheless, to finance his expeditions, he must keep this image unblemished. Solid as pack ice. What government can refuse to fund a living legend? What private investor does not benefit from association with him?"

"What he did to you was a tragedy — but to Peary, it was bad publicity," Dob continues. "And he is a master of publicity. First he keeps himself out of the States, where he might be challenged. Then, taking precious time from his terribly important exploration, he crafts a sincere, well-wrought letter to the newspaper, nobly 'taking full responsibility.' That, of course, is his last comment on the matter, which is left by default in the hands of the Museum of Natural History!"

"But it was the *museum*, not Peary, that took my father's body away!" I reply.

Dob nods. "And they should be taken to task. But you see, Minik, it is *Peary* who has the power to send you back home."

"Perhaps you can appeal to his Christian charity," says the priest.

"Peary's charity extends to the Church of Peary and no further," Dob replies. "I believe it will take publicity. I told you that before you left, Minik — that is why we set up that interview with the *Examiner*. You could have waited for that to be published before traipsing up to Canada! *I've* been squawking to the press on your behalf this month, too, by God! Er, pardon me, Father."

Miss Tilley clears her throat. "Chester, your manners —"

"Dob, it won't do any good," I say. "Peary won't read it all the way in the Arctic."

"But his wife is in New York," Dob says. "She covers his affairs like a hawk. Both she and he would like nothing more than for the case of Minik Wallace to disappear. And these articles will do just the opposite — *just what he wants least!* The more we throw at him, you see, the more we'll get. The public has heard the story of your father. Somehow Peary has weathered that so far, but we will of course hammer it home from coast to coast. But if we had something more, some new chink in the Peary armor —"

I do see.

I see very clearly.

I have been a fool. All along I have been playing directly into the hands of Robert Peary. Everything I have done recently — fleeing New York with no money, contracting pneumonia, putting my fate in the hands of strangers, attempting suicide — Peary could not have planned it better himself.

"'How convenient that no one can *see* what he does in the Arctic' — isn't that what you said, Miss Tilley?"

"I believe you may be paraphrasing," she replies, "but yes, that is the gist."

How convenient.

How very convenient indeed.

Peary's reputation may be solid as pack ice. But even pack ice, with the right pressure, can crack.

Out of curiosity, I feel the side of my head. The bump is still there.

Inussuanga.

I know exactly what to do.

Blackmail

"Very good to see you; thank you for coming!" says Miss Tilley to the *World* reporter, then politely closes the door to Dob's suite at the Hotel Astor behind him. She turns with a devilish smile. "Well, how was it? Did you give it to Peary?"

I smile. "I just told the truth. That's all."

"*The New York Times,* the *World,* the *Evening Mail* . . . you must be exhausted!"

"Not as much as you appear to be."

"Well! It's a good thing Mr. Beecroft is a professional publicist. The reporters are *flocking* here. Then again, I suppose the story itself is not hard to sell."

The door flies open and Dob rushes in. "Oh, my boy! Are you sitting down? You are a *genius!*" I have never seen Dob so excited. He is brandishing a newspaper. "A two-page spread, Minik! We couldn't have *bought* publicity like this."

He lays an open copy of the *San Francisco Examiner* on the living room coffee table. The sight of it makes me flinch. On the right-hand page is a dreadful drawing of a dark young man in knickers — obviously meant to represent me — striking a pose of horror in front of a glass case containing a skeleton, at whose feet is a placard reading: SKELETON OF AN ESKIMO PRESENTED BY ROBERT PEARY.

"But my father's skeleton was never on display," I say. "The bones are in storage."

Dob shrugs. "Ah well, it's about time someone stretched the truth on your behalf."

The headline spans both pages:

Why Arctic Explorer Peary's Neglected Eskimo Boy Wants to Shoot Him

The pathetic appeal of little Mene Wallace, who was brought to New York "in the interest of science," turned adrift after all his unhappy relatives had died here and he had seen his father's skeleton grin at him from a glass case in the Museum of Natural History, and who has abandoned "civilization" because he cannot get justice

When Commander Robert E. Peary returned in 1897 from one of his expeditions into the Arctic he brought back to New York five Eskimos "in the interest of science."

"I told the reporter *six* Eskimos," I say.

Dob is pacing the room, shaking his head. "To think, you gave this brilliant interview before you left — and you almost wasted it by trying to . . . Well, go on!"

I read aloud:

"'All of these unfortunates are dead except one — a little Eskimo lad now nineteen years old and called Mene Wallace.

"'Now this lad, long since abandoned to his own devices by Peary, who refused to take him back to the North when he called last year, rescued from the Museum of Natural History, and since living upon the charity of his few friends, has run away. He was driven by a double desire to return to his Greenland home and seek redress from the explorer.

"'This poor, outraged little savage has learned to speak English with remarkable fluency . . .'"

I skim the rest. The bulk of the piece is my interview, which has been given the byline *By Mene Wallace, Last Survivor of Peary's Wretched Eskimos.*

Dob looks over my shoulder. "Did you really say, 'I would shoot Mr. Peary and the Museum director, only I want them to see how much more civilized just a savage Eskimo is than their enlightened white selves'?"

"I was angry," I reply.

"Ha! Inspired!" Dob claps me on the back. "Well, already we are seeing some encouraging results. I have just spoken to the Danish consul, who has been following your case for a while, and he is *extremely* interested in these latest developments. And I have received word from none other than Mrs. Peary. She has been vexed by the *Examiner* article —"

"Hell hath no fury like a woman scorned," says Miss Tilley.

"In addition," Dob says with an impish smile, "I have the news we have all been waiting for."

"The child?" Miss Tilley says. "Peary's child?"

"A boy," Dob replies. "Kaalipaluk. Born three years ago . . . on board the *Roosevelt!*"

"And the mother . . . was it Aleqasina?" I ask.

"Sounds right, old fellow, but I have a dreadful time with those names." Dob hands me my coat. "I believe Mrs. Peary has always suspected this. And I have just gotten word that she would like to see us, posthaste. I have invited your Uncle Will to join us. Hoo hoo! There is a relief ship for Peary leaving in a month's time — and you, dear chum, will be on it!"

"Dob, I need to think about this," I say.

"Oh, good God, Minik, this is your ticket."

"But the Eskimos — offering wives — it's a tradition, not a sin the way it is here —" I stammer. "It's —"

"Blackmail?" says Dob brightly. "It's the least we can do."

The Peary Arctic Club occupies a small brick building on East Seventieth Street. A stuffed bear greets us inside the front door, looking rather upset by his adopted habitat of polished oak walls, brass spittoons, and thick red leather armchairs. The smell of tobacco seems to have displaced much of the oxygen, and a chandelier fashioned of antlers and electric lightbulbs does not do much to dispel the gloom.

Great fuss is made over allowing Miss Tilley into a men's club, but the attendant eventually leads us up a wide staircase to a second-floor landing. A door is open to our right, and we are ushered into a large common room with shuttered windows and a roaring fireplace.

"Ah, Mene, let me take a look at you!" A walrus of a man approaches across the faded carpet, his footsteps springy and light for a man his size. I have met Herbert Bridgman before, mostly in the company of Mr. Jesup. He is gray now but fit and barrel-chested, with a deep cleft in his chin and mustaches that resemble the cowcatcher on the front of a locomotive. "A fine young man — *kussanna!*"

The word, for *handsome,* has clearly taken a feat of memorization. I bow gratefully and reply, "*Avataq.*"

It means *seal bladder,* but Mr. Bridgman smiles with gratitude.

Mrs. Peary rises from her chair stiffly. Her eyes are unwavering, her thin lips yielding just slightly from the horizontal into a smile. "Mene," she says with a bow. "Mr. Beecroft. Mr. Wallace. And . . . I don't believe we've met, madam?"

"Perhaps across the footlights. Tilley. Vesta Tilley."

"Of course."

The attendant has pulled up seats for us around a wooden table in front of the fireplace. Mrs. Peary does not offer her hand to any of us. When she sits, we sit.

"To the point, then," Mr. Bridgman says. "As you may remember, Wallace, back in 'ninety-nine, I was the one who first suggested that Mene come north with me on a summer supply ship to Greenland."

"Yes," Uncle Will says. "But he was too ill at the time to travel."

"After which, by all accounts, he became a beloved member of the Wallace family and took wonderfully to life here in New York. Isn't that true, Mene?"

"I was happy with Uncle Will."

"Well — there, then! What is all this fuss now about revenge and returning home? An educated young man like you, Mene, retreating to a life of deprivation and illiteracy? Tell me, do you remember your language?"

It is a good question. I have not spoken more than a few Eskimo words to anyone in years. "I suppose I could pick it up. . . ."

"From whom? Do you have family to return to?"

"No."

"Tell me, Mene, do you fancy raw seal? Because that's about all they eat up there."

"I, uh . . ." The truth is, I don't remember what it tastes like.

"Not to mention *kivioq* — you recall that? Dead auks sewn into a seal intestine and left for two months to rot. Eaten raw, remember? The Eskimos say it's like candy!"

"Herbert, please," mutters Mrs. Peary.

"Could you fend for yourself — wait by the breathing hole for a seal with your harpoon, stalk a polar bear who may also be stalking you in the blinding snow, hunt a walrus? Because you'll need those skills to survive. The nearest vegetable and fruit market would be . . . Copenhagen, I suppose."

I look at Dob and Uncle Will. They seem as much at a loss for words as I am. "I will need to relearn some skills," I admit.

"Oh, I daresay yes," Mr. Bridgman replies. "Especially considering your skills and your language development were those of an eight-year-old when you left. And as you know, the Eskimos do not take kindly to an adult tribe member who does not pull his weight."

"My dear Mr. Bridgman," says Miss Tilley, "do I detect a threatening tone?"

"I am merely concerned for the boy's welfare. And I have a proposition." Mr. Bridgman sits in an easy chair and lights up a pipe. "I will help — in a concrete, constructive way. I will agree to spread the word among my many colleagues, inquiring about a job for a strong young man — perhaps something in New England — cold country — logging or road building, near a town with a good library. Sound good?"

"And in return?" I ask.

"You allow a printed retraction to everything you said, then drop all contact with the press."

I have not come expecting this. But Mr. Bridgman may be right. How *will* I adjust? I am a New Yorker now. I remember *seeing* my father kill a seal, but I haven't the foggiest idea how to do it myself. I love steak, medium well-done. I eat pork roast and lamb chops.

But . . . raw seal? *Kivioq?*

"Steady, Minik," whispers Dob.

"I object, Mr. Bridgman!" Miss Tilley says. "You have done your best to thoroughly intimidate this young man, and I am outraged —"

"The footlights are off, Miss Tilley," interrupts Mrs. Peary. "And tell me, these threats to my husband in the national press, what would you call them if not intimidation?"

Uncle Will finally speaks up. "Your husband is an extraordinary man. His bravery is unmatched, and the country will forever be in debt for his discoveries. Surely, with all his organizational skills, he can arrange for a voyage north for this young man."

"It is expensive to mount a relief ship, and there is never enough room for even the essentials," Mrs. Peary says. "Even so, Mene has been given opportunities to go home throughout his life. He turned them all down."

"Others were making decisions for me then," I explain. "I am a man now. I would like passage on the *Jeannie*. I will work to earn my keep."

Mrs. Peary's jaw tightens. "I am afraid not. For one thing, the ship is already so far over capacity that *I* cannot board. And even if it were not . . . you accuse my husband of all manner of despicable crimes while he is not here to defend himself, and then announce to the entire country that you intend to shoot him — and you expect me to grant this wish? With all respect to the company present, I will be blackmailed over my dead body. Mr. Bridgman, lead them out."

Dob leaps to his feet. "Mrs. Peary, no offense meant to

you, but when I see your husband I will tell the truth to his face — that he is a scoundrel, a liar, a slave driver, and an adulterer!"

"A *what*?" Mrs. Peary says.

"See here, Mr. Beecroft!" Mr. Bridgman steps in front of him.

But Dob is turning quickly the color of the hearth flames. "How long before a photograph of the little one is revealed? Who will notice the features on the baby's face — those remorseless blue eyes set in the skin of an Eskimo —"

"Dob . . ." I grab his arm and pull him away. Uncle Will closes behind me, blocking Dob from Mr. Bridgman, whose fists are clenched.

Miss Tilley is at the door, fanning herself.

All I want to do is leave. Once again, everything has gone wrong. I realize now that I have just sealed my fate. I will be in New York forever.

No matter what I do, I cause pain and chaos to everyone around me. I can't bear it. I want it to stop.

The ring of a telephone in the corner breaks the silence. Mr. Bridgman turns away. I look over to Mrs. Peary, who has sunk into a leather chair.

I walk to her and kneel. "Mrs. Peary, I am truly sorry. I will never, ever say a word or do anything to hurt you or your husband."

"Minik —" Dob sputters.

"Neither will Mr. Beecroft or Miss Tilley," I continue. "I promise."

She does not reply, but I do not expect her to.

129

The attendant, who has entered the room to answer the telephone, now calls out, "Mr. Bridgman, for you. The Danish consul."

Mr. Bridgman's eyes are on me as he takes the receiver. "You're a good man, Mene," he says, "but I would choose my associates more carefully in the future. Yours have, alas, done you in."

Dob is standing by the doorway, trembling. I take him by the arm, and we leave.

Home

"'Courtesy of the Peary Arctic Club,'" Uncle Will reads from a sheet he has pulled from a box that has arrived by postal messenger.

I pull out two small leather bags. They are a medical kit and a set of dentist's tools.

We both stare at them for a moment, then burst out laughing. "Extending the frontiers of twentieth-century science to Smith Sound," says Uncle Will.

I close the kits and shove them into my suitcase. I have packed selectively — one pair of leather boots, although I know I will learn to make *kamiks,* polar-bearskin boots; a wool hat; my favorite full-length overcoat, given to me by the priest; volumes of Dickens, Thackeray, Fielding, and Melville; and, of course, candy and peanuts.

I will undoubtedly throw most of it away, but for a while it will remind me of my life in New York.

"The carriage will arrive in an hour," says Uncle Will. His voice is subdued.

It is July, and I have had nearly two months to adjust. But it still seems too bizarre to be real.

When I left the Peary Arctic Club, I was speechless,

devastated. Dob kept trying to cheer me up with vows that he would continue the fight. "Bridgman is nothing more than a glorified secretary and bodyguard, anyway," he claimed.

Dob treated me to a night at the theater, seeing Miss Tilley, who introduced me to the entire audience. I had adjusted to the idea of staying in New York and begun inquiries into working on the new subway system, laying track.

After a week spent on the receiving end of baleful stares and cutting comments from workers, I came home to a telegraph from Mr. Bridgman: OPENING HAS ARISEN ON BOARD *JEANNIE* STOP OFFER CREW POSITION TO MENE STOP IMMEDIATE REPLY REQUESTED.

And that was that. No explanation, no visit.

Naturally Uncle Will and I made a call at East Seventieth Street to say thanks, but neither Mr. Bridgman nor Mrs. Peary was there. We left a message but have not heard back.

I will never know what changed their minds. Dob is convinced his threat worked. Miss Tilley assumed it was the call from the Danish consul. Uncle Will believes that my kindness to Mrs. Peary softened her.

I will never know.

Miss Tilley has begun writing a one-woman play about the subject. She intends to play Mrs. Peary. I am rather glad that if and when this is ever produced, I will be long gone.

I will admit I am afraid. I do not know if anyone in Smith Sound will remember me. I wonder if they will welcome me as a returning villager or shun me for leaving. I wonder if I will like them.

I wonder if they will like me.

In the past few weeks I have had little sleep. My father has visited me in my dreams once or twice, but I can never quite understand what he is trying to say. Perhaps as I get closer to home, I will know.

May the living return to the land they hold dear. I think of my father's song often. In the end those words have guided me.

I know I am doing the right thing.

Still, leaving Uncle Will is terribly hard. He is avoiding eye contact. He sniffles often, making excuses about a summer cold. He has continued to apologize at least a thousand times for the wrongs he has committed.

I have forgiven him. I hope that others do, too, for the wrongs he committed at the museum.

From out front comes the hollow pounding of horses' hooves. As I grab my suitcase, Uncle Will runs to the window and looks out. "Not yet," he says. "These are visitors!"

He pulls open the door and hurries outside.

Visitors, on the day we are to say good-bye? I follow him to a large carriage that has pulled up to the lawn.

A young man in his early twenties emerges. He has broad shoulders and a bit of a belly. "Well, well," he says, "if it isn't my old stepbrother, looking like a Connecticut Yankee in King Qisuk's Igloo!"

It takes me a moment to realize who it is.

"Willie!" I nearly fall over the front stoop running to embrace him. "You got so fat! Congratulations!"

"It will happen to you, too, when you get married and sit around the house eating, in utter bliss." He turns to help a lovely and very pregnant raven-haired young lady out of the carriage.

I feel my jaw drop to my chest. The years have only perfected what seemed perfect in the first place. "Hell —" The word catches in my throat. "Hello, Matilda."

Willie shakes his head. "The fantods. Even at this age."

"Oh, Minik," Matilda says, "how can we apologize enough for not having seen you in all these years?" She wraps her arms around me, but her bulging abdomen gets in the way.

"Well, I see you've been busy," I remark.

"I'm due this week," she says shyly.

"If it's a boy, name it Qisuk!" I blurt out.

"We'll take that under advisement," Willie says, looking up the street. "Say, when is your carriage coming?"

"Fifteen minutes," Uncle Will replies.

"Let my driver take you instead," Willie suggests. "Matilda will have to stay and rest, of course, but you and I can talk about old times — and I can give you marriage advice, which you can use in Greenland. They do marry in Greenland, don't they?"

"Oh!" Matilda exclaims. "I brought something for you."

She reaches into her bag and hands me a small wrapped box.

"Thank you."

"Open it, right here!"

I untie the red ribbon, then carefully unfold the paper and remove the box lid. Inside is the oddest-looking figure I have seen, sewn together from what look like scraps of cloth and scorched leather.

I pull it out into the light.

And I look into a face I have mourned since I was a boy. Qunualuq.

I hold him to my face and breathe in. Through the faint stink of old gunpowder, I can smell the world of my child-hood — hunting, kayaks, icebergs, the beast, the biscuits, *Ahnighito*. It all rushes back to me. "How — where did you — ?"

"The day I blew him up, I collected all the scraps I could," Willie says. "I kept going back to look. I vowed I would find all of him and make Qunualuq like new."

"He didn't, of course," Matilda adds, "and he gave up on the idea. But when we were married, I found the scraps in his drawer. I told him we should reconstruct your old companion — just fill in the blanks with materials from our house."

"He's changed, huh?" asks Willie.

He has. He looks odd in this new part-Eskimo, part-American form.

But he is still Qunualuq, still Smiler.

"His soul," I reply, "is the same."

We have little time for good-byes. And it is truly sad to see Uncle Will cry for the first time.

But as I head away across the Macombs Dam Bridge, I

135

realize how much smaller it seems to me than it did a few years ago. How much of the landscape I have memorized. How the smell of the air, which was once so close and suffocating, now seems fresh and familiar.

We keep up a steady stream of talk down Broadway, remarking on the feverish pace of building that has reached even this rural corner of the island. And as we travel down the West Drive of the park, just outside the Museum of Natural History, I lean close to the window and look to my left.

The tree canopies are a lush summer green, but as we pass over a bridge I hold Qunualuq up to the window and I squint. For a moment, in the glare of the morning light, the lake looks like a vast bay, its bank a rocky shore.

"What are you looking at?" Willie says with a laugh.

"Nothing," I say.

But it's there. I see it.

It looks like home.

Author's Note

We weren't looking for Minik.

We were on vacation, on the way to a mountain hike in a remote area of Vermont called the Northeast Kingdom — where granite mountains give way to ice-blue glacial lakes, where roads twist and then suddenly disappear, where names like Lake Memphremagog come easily off the tongue and anything below the Kancamagus Highway is the distant south.

My wife, Tina, was driving. I was driving her crazy, bellowing out the oddest names I could find on the map — "Next stop, Ticklenaked Pond!"

I'd left Minik home. Which was a good thing, because he'd become an obsession. A year or so earlier, I'd read the only book ever written about him, the excellent biography by Kenn Harper called *Give Me My Father's Body*. It isn't often that a book turns me inside out, but this one did. Any writer worth his or her salt is always on the lookout for The Story — the one that hasn't been told. I knew, somehow, I'd found mine.

Not the history of Minik's life. That had already been told, far better than I could have done. What hooked me was the other story — the unknown one. The story of how it feels to see a city emerge from the fog when you've never in your life even seen a tree. To be put on display before a procession of thirty thousand people. To watch as your entire family slowly succumbs to diseases that did not exist in your world. To grow up, play, go to school, and fall in love, not just as a member of a minority group, but as the only one. To discover, at age fifteen, that the most important event of your life was a fraud, and the person you loved most was part of it. To desperately seek a way home and find all routes closed.

It was a story that spoke to our own times, too, I thought — and I wanted to try to find not only the facts that support the life, but the life that supports the facts.

Over time, *Smiler's Bones* would emerge. It is a novel. Although it uses history as a framework, many of the incidents are made up. Peary did dump biscuits, shout *"Kiiha Takeqihunga,"* and steal Ahnighito with hydraulic jacks. The newspaper articles are direct quotes. Minik did shoot an owl and run away from home and contemplate suicide and threaten Peary in the press, and he was indeed rescued by Dob and Vesta Tilley. He did not, as far as I know, misbehave so violently toward Mr. Jesup, play baseball against a team called the Duyvils, fall in love with a girl named Matilda, have a doll called Qunualuq, or see Qisuk's ghost. These incidents came from my imagination and were subject to two tests: They had to be things, based in research, that *could* have happened during the gaps in the historical record; and they had to shed light on who Minik was *inside*, to the best of my knowledge.

But on that August day on that road in northern Vermont, none of this had yet been written. All of it was far away — three hundred miles away.

"To our left . . . Coaticook!" I called out to Tina.

"Um, do you have any idea where we're going?" she asked.

I thought I did. But Minik had an odd way of calling when I least expected. In the back of my mind I knew he'd lived the last years of his life in New England. In truth, although *Smiler's Bones* has a triumphant ending, Minik's return to Greenland was anything but. He was caught between two cultures. As an educated New Yorker, he found it impossible to fit into his native society — and years later, after a broken marriage and failed friendships, he returned to the States. He found a job working in a New Hampshire logging camp and a measure of happiness living with a family named Hall. He never did get back his father's bones. In 1918 the Spanish influenza swept through the camp, killing almost all of the workers, including Minik. Just twenty-seven years old, he was buried in a tiny village called Pittsburg.

PITTSBURG, NEW HAMPSHIRE . . .

There it was — on my map, east of Coaticook and west of Magalloway Mountain, seventy miles away. "You won't believe this . . ." I began, explaining what I'd discovered.

Tina listened patiently and smiled. "What are we waiting for?" she said.

Our hiking plans went out the window. We were on a quest to find Minik's grave.

Two hours later we pulled into the empty parking lot of

the whitewashed Pittsburg Historical Society building. The place was closed, but an energetic older couple, Carolyn and Captain Stuart Drew, had stopped in to tidy up. I told them about my book and our search, and soon Tina and I were off with a handful of materials and careful directions.

From a distance, the tiny Indian Stream Cemetery doesn't look like it can possibly contain the remains of generations of an entire village. But it does, in family plots that span centuries, and we almost gave up finding Minik — until Tina's surprised scream brought me running. Squeezed into an odd corner too small for a plot, his body marked by a simple flat granite slab, was MENE WALLACE.

A small, modern-looking statue and some hideous fake flowers had given him away. Not nearly as dignified and staid as the American flags and small bouquets that decorated the other graves. It was as if Minik was in the back of the class, laughing. Still different. And proud ot it.

We sat nearby and talked silently to him for a while. In my hand was a copy of the Pittsburg *Town Clerk and Personal Records November 1906 to 1920* by one Sylvester Lyford. A typical set of entries: *Apr. 2, 1907 — Whit Terrill put Elsie Gay out of his house . . . Apr. 3 — Henry Terrill got drunk on rum at Bessie Heath's . . . Apr. 5 — Whit Terrill Sobered up . . . Apr. 6 — Henry Terrill Sobered up . . .*

We flipped through the purchases and family dramas, the murders and fires and births, looking for any mention of Minik, the celebrity who had been the center of a national scandal involving the most sensational exploration of his time. He was mentioned once:

Oct. 29, 1918 — The Eskimo died at Fred Halls place.

"Well," I said to Tina, "at least someone took the trouble to give him a decent burial."

I had read that Smiler's bones had indeed been finally put to rest. In 1993, bowing to pressure, the American Museum of Natural History released them to the Polar Eskimos of Greenland. Ironically in the end, Minik hadn't had the privilege of a return home that his father had. No ceremony, no press coverage, not even much of a marker. Just plastic flowers and a forgotten corner of the earth.

But as we ate our lunches silently, the wind bending the grass and the stream lapping beyond the fence, just as they had been doing for the eighty-five years since Minik arrived, I changed my mind.

Qisuk, I realized, belonged in Greenland. Leaving it had killed him.

Minik, who had lived both in Greenland and New York City, belonged to neither. That was how I'd thought of him, a boy without a home.

But he'd called to us that day, to show us we were wrong. It hadn't all been bad, he was saying — *look where I ended up!* It wasn't Smith Sound, but it sure wasn't the Bronx, either. I'd be lucky to do as well someday.

He was in the breeze, in the song of the birds, and the rush of the current. I thought I could see him smiling, perfectly happy just where he was.

Peter Lerangis, July 2004

143

Bibliography

BOOKS

Berton, Pierre. *The Arctic Grail: The Quest for the Northwest Passage and the North Pole, 1818–1909.* New York: Viking Penguin, 1988.

Burrows, Edwin G., and Mike Wallace. *Gotham: A History of New York City to 1898.* New York: Oxford University Press, 1999.

Counter, S. Allen. *North Pole Legacy: Black, White, and Eskimo.* Amherst, MA: University of Massachusetts Press, 1991.

Ehrlich, Gretel. *This Cold Heaven: Seven Seasons in Greenland.* New York: Pantheon Books, 2001.

Field, Edward (based on songs and stories collected by Knud Rasmussen). *Magic Words.* New York: Gulliver Books, Harcourt Brace, 1998.

Harper, Kenn. *Give Me My Father's Body: The Life of Minik, the New York Eskimo.* South Royalton, VT: Steerforth Press, 2000.

Jackson, Kenneth T. (ed.). *The Encyclopedia of New York City.* New Haven, CT: Yale University Press, 1995.

Johnston, Wayne. *The Navigator of New York*. New York: Doubleday, 2002.

Kouwenhoven, John A. *The Columbia Historical Portrait of New York*. Garden City, NY: Doubleday, 1953.

Kpomassie, Tété-Michel. *An African in Greenland*. New York: New York Review of Books, 1981.

Lopez, Barry. *Arctic Dreams*. New York: Vintage Books/ Random House, 1986.

Lowenstein, Tom (tr., from material originally collected by Knud Rasmussen). *Eskimo Poems from Canada and Greenland*. Pittsburgh, PA: University of Pittsburgh Press, 1973.

Morrison, David, and Georges-Hébert Germain. *Inuit: Glimpses of an Arctic Past*. Quebec: Canadian Museum of Civilization, 1995.

Norman, Howard (ed.). *Northern Tales: Stories from the Native Peoples of the Arctic and Subarctic Regions*. New York: Pantheon Books, 1990.

Preston, Douglas J. *Dinosaurs in the Attic: An Excursion into the American Museum of Natural History*. New York: St. Martin's Press, 1986.

Swadesh, Morris. "Linguistic Structures of Native America: South Greenlandic (Eskimo)." *Viking Fund Publications in Anthropology*, 6. New York: Viking Press, 1946.

Thomas, David Hurst. *Skull Wars: Kenniwick Man, Archaeology, and the Battle for Native American Identity*. New York: Basic Books, 2000.

FILMS

(All of these have scenes of disturbing violence and mature subject matters, which may not be suitable for pre-teen viewers.)

Atanarjuat (English title: *The Fast Runner*), in Inuit with English subtitles, Zacharias Kunuk (dir.). Igloolik Isuma Productions/The National Film Board of Canada, Igloolik, Nunavut, Canada, 2001. A bleak, exhilarating drama of Shakespearean dimensions, based on an oral legend dating back several centuries, made by a production company that is seventy-five percent Inuit-owned.

Lysets hjerte (Inuit title: *Qaamarngup Uummataa*; English title: *Heart of Light*), in Inuit with English subtitles, Jacob Grønlykke (dir.). ASA Film Production, Copenhagen, Denmark, 1998. A modern drama, the first major production filmed completely in Greenland.

Nanook of the North, silent film made in 1922 with text, restored in 1998 with a musical score, Robert J. Flaherty (dir.). Kino on Video, New York, 1998. Although controversial for its reenactments of forgotten and outmoded customs, this is generally considered to be the first documentary film ever made — and by many accounts, one of the best.

The White Dawn, Philip Kaufman (dir.), based on the novel by James Houston. Paramount Pictures, 1974.

AFTER WORDS™

PETER LERANGIS'S

Smiler's Bones

CONTENTS

About the Author

Q&A with Peter Lerangis

21 Things You Might Not Have Known About Greenland

After Words™ guide by Ranya Fattouh

About the Author

Peter Lerangis is the author of more than 140 books for early readers through teens, which have sold over 2.5 million copies. *Smiler's Bones* has enjoyed great critical success, called "hugely fascinating," "vivid," and "brilliant" by *Kirkus Reviews*, "wrenching" by *Booklist*, and "unforgettable" by *School Library Journal*. It was a Junior Library Guild selection and made the New York Public Library Books for the Teen Age 2006 and Bank Street Best Books of 2006 lists.

Peter's unusual life experiences — Harvard graduate with a degree in biochemistry, Broadway musical theater actor/singer, marathon runner, father of two sons — are evident in his range and in his intelligent, humorous, fast-paced writing. His gripping mystery series, Spy X, has sold a million copies. In September 2003, First Lady Laura Bush selected him along with two other writers, Marc Brown and R. L. Stine, to accompany her to Moscow to represent the United States in the first Russian Book Festival. The following year, the National Book Foundation chose him to be a Family Literacy Writer-in-Residence. In 2001, Peter's two-book polar adventure, Antarctica, was selected as required reading by the JASON organization. Two books in his sci-fi/mystery series, Watchers, were cited by the American Library Association for its 1999 Quick Picks for Reluctant Readers and by the Children's Book Council/International Reading Association for its 2000 Children's Choice Books.

Peter Lerangis is one of the country's most in-demand

movie novelization authors, having adapted *The Sixth Sense* and *Batman Begins*, among many others. He also enjoys visiting schools to talk about the writer's life, communicating an infectious enthusiasm and an inspiring love of words and the writing craft.

Q&A with Peter Lerangis

Q: *What were some of your favorite books growing up, and who were your literary influences?*

A: DC Comics were big, especially Superman. I was a fat, bookish kid who basically read everything he could get his hands on. I devoured a series of orange-covered adventures of Tom Swift. I liked big life-or-death books and science fiction. *1984* really turned me inside out, and I couldn't read enough Ray Bradbury and Edgar Allan Poe. But it was a Jack London story, "To Build a Fire," that changed my life. Reading it, I had an almost out-of-body experience — shivers, cold, distance, dislocation, the works. It shocked me that words could do that. I left my room in a kind of daze and tried to explain this to my dad but I couldn't, it was too personal. I knew I wanted to do what London did: take people out of their ordinary lives and make them feel something unexpected and powerful. Eventually, when I became a dad and began reading to my own sons, I was in the middle of *Ferdinand* (remember that — the bull who wanted to just sit and smell the flowers?), when I choked up and couldn't continue reading. Something deep and emotional in that simple book had stayed with me all those decades. I'm constantly rediscovering books that were important to me.

Q: *When did you become a writer? You've led such a diverse life — scientist, musical theater actor, parent — why and how did you settle on writing as a profession?*

A: I had to put aside a lot of confusion and fear. You know the prince in *Monty Python and the Holy Grail* who surveys his future kingdom and says, "But father, all I want to do is sing!" That was me, without the toga (or the kingdom). All I ever wanted to do was write stories and perform on stage. Where I grew up, no one did those kinds of things for a living. I was the oldest kid in a big Greek-American family, and a lot was expected of me (read: doctor, scientist, lawyer, businessman). I tried them one by one. I majored in biochemistry in college, but I didn't have the desire to be a doctor or researcher, so after graduation I worked in a Wall Street law firm and applied to law school.

Being in New York was exhilarating — but I was happiest *after* work, when I was going to the theater, taking voice lessons, writing in a journal on my train ride home. My old passions tugged at me until I had to give in. I quit the job, deferred law school, traveled across the country with friends in a beat-up Chevy, spent the summer as a singing waiter on Nantucket Island, and then stormed New York City on shaky legs, determined to be an actor. I was so afraid of chickening out that I made myself go to an audition right away, without a picture, a résumé, or music — just my name scribbled on a torn-out piece of notebook paper.

I got the show, and I was finally doing something I wanted to do! I spent eight years or so doing plays all across the country, including a long tour with a Broadway show. Between gigs, I kept getting fired from waiting jobs, so I faked a résumé and became a freelance editor at publishing houses in NYC, which really felt like home. I began writing again. Being an author was wonderful; I didn't have to audition or leave home for weeks at a time, and I could tell my own stories rather than someone else's. I made the switch, and I haven't looked back since.

Q: *What in particular attracted you to this story, these characters, and this "little chunk of history"?*
A: It was that sad little face, staring out of a book review of Kenn Harper's amazing *Give Me My Father's Body*. I don't know why I felt such an overpowering connection to him. I could say I share the feeling of being an outsider, but that trivializes his life. I also love stories set in old New York, and the American Museum of Natural History has been like a second home to my sons and me, but that's only a part of it, too. Father–son stories always move me, and this one has two of them, both ending in betrayals. But it was really something more and less than all of those things, something deep and instinctive and mysterious that just said *write me*.

Q: *You studied science in college and were considering becoming a scientist at one point in your life. As a former student of science, do you agree with the museum's decision to study these Eskimos?*
A: Yes! And no! It's nearly impossible to look at the world through late-nineteenth-century eyes. People like Boas, whose actions seem clueless to us now, have to be understood in context. They were at the cutting edge of anthropology. When the old-school scientists were saying that Eskimos and Aborigines and Native Americans were further down the evolutionary ladder, with inferior and undeveloped brains, Boas

kicked and screamed. He and his colleagues were trying to show that aboriginal people were *identical* to so-called "civilized people." The new-school anthropologists would sometimes travel to far-flung parts of the world and live with the tribes to see what their lives were like. This was radical. And it changed forever the way people of different cultures interrelate.

But the anthropologists' flaw, which is obvious to us, wasn't so clear to them. In their eagerness to enlighten the public, they believed it was necessary to bring the aboriginals to "civilization." How else could civilized society know about the richness and sophistication of the distant cultures? Germ theory was in its infancy; sickness was still a quasi-mystical condition brought about by "humours." The idea that the aboriginals would feel dislocated or uncomfortable — well, those things would yield to politeness and courtesy, and they were temporary anyway, because soon the people would be shipped home. Could the scientists have known this treatment was dehumanizing and would lead to the devastation of a little boy's life? Could they have done things differently? Probably. What happened to Minik was unforgivable. But it's important to know that the players in this story were humans, not monsters.

Q: *The scene where Willie steals Minik's Qunualuq (doll) is very powerful. Where did you get the idea for this scene?*
A: My older son, Nick, had a "dolly" that went wherever he did. It was made for him by a good friend, Sarah Weeks, the children's book author, and he's had Dolly since the day he

was born. He held her a certain way to help him sleep, and whenever she fell behind the bed he was distressed. When she became threadbare and Sarah made him a new one, he rejected it. It had to be the old dolly. One day, when he dropped her on a New York City sidewalk, miles from our building, my wife went on a search for her, just as devastated as our son. When she found Dolly she burst into tears. Dolly has always been a life force. To this day, at age nineteen, Nick still takes comfort from her (but not when anyone is looking). I hadn't thought of Qunualuq until I started researching Inuit art and culture. When I learned that mothers would sew sealskin dolls, I knew just what to do.

Q: *You chose to write a different ending for Minik than what really happened to him. Can you explain your choice?*

A: Actually, it did really happen to him. He did return to Greenland in the manner described in *Smiler's Bones.* I chose to leave out the later part of his life, his adult experiences in Greenland. I wanted to examine Minik's youth, his coming of age, not his adulthood. Minik's departure for Greenland was the natural stopping point, a triumphant transitional moment marking the end of his youth. A novel has different demands than a biography; it needs a novel's scope. Going further would have felt like another story. I included an explanation of Minik's adult life in the afterword, which I melded with the tale of how my wife and I found Minik's grave. Minik lived to be twenty-seven, and his adult years in Greenland (and eventually New Hampshire) were grueling, sad, and short — definitely material for a novel, but not this one.

Q: *In the very last chapter, Willie and Matilda give Minik a repaired Qunualuq, and though the doll's appearance has changed, its soul has not. Is there a parallel between Minik's transformation and his doll's transformation?*

A: Yes, absolutely. Like Minik, he is a patchwork, "part-American and part-Eskimo." He's been blown apart but has kept himself together. He is a survivor.

Q: *What other parts of history do you find yourself drawn to? Would you ever write another historically based novel and, if so, what subject would you write on?*

A: I love urban stories. I think cities not only bring out the best and worst in people, but they *are* human in the way they grow, decay, reflect, coddle, and devour. I've had my eye on a story that revolves around a shocking but little-known event that occurred in New York City in the 1700s.

21 Things You Might Not Have Known About Greenland

1. Greenland got its name not because it has lush green fields (as its name implies), but because people were purposely misled to believe that it was a good place to grow crops to make a good living. Viking explorers in the Arctic Circle started the lie about the frozen island in order to attract settlers who otherwise might have been scared off. Long after the Vikings had passed and their subterfuge had been discovered, the erroneous label remained as the island's name.

2. Greenland was claimed as territory by the country of Denmark for many years. It is now a self-governing territory but is technically still a part of Denmark.

3. Greenland shouldn't even be called Greenland anymore. The correct name of the now independent country is Kalaallit Nunaat (meaning "The Humans' Land").

4. The Greenland shark is one of the largest sharks in the world and is the largest arctic fish.

5. Greeland's culture has much in common with Inuit tradition, since the majority of its people are descended from Inuit. Many people still go ice fishing and there are annual dog-sled races.

6. Erik the Red set sail for Greenland in 986, eventually arriving with fourteen boats and establishing two farming settlements on the east coast of the island. He is considered the first mainlander to "discover"

Greenland. The settlement he established there was the first European settlement in the New World.

7. At 840,000 square miles, Greenland is the largest island in the world. It is three times the size of Texas.

8. Most Greenlanders speak Greenlandic (Kalaallisut) as their first language. It is spoken by about 50,000 people.

9. European football (known as soccer in the United States) is the national sport of Greenland, but Greenland is not a member of the International Football Association, since the international organization requires that fields have natural grass, which is impossible in Greenland's climate.

10. A two-mile-thick dome of glacial ice covers most of Greenland. The weight of the ice is so great that if it suddenly melted, the bedrock of the island would rise 2,500 feet!

11. Traditional Greenlandic music includes sacred drum dances played on an oval drum made of a wooden frame with a bear bladder. The drum dances are based around a single dancer, who composes songs sung by his family while he dances, usually in a qaggi, a snow house built specifically for community events such as this. A drum dancer's skills are evaluated by his endurance in his lengthy performance and the nature of his compositions. Drum dances are an important element of Greenlandic Inuit cultural cohesion, and function as personal expression, pure entertainment, and social sanction.

12. There is plenty of light in Greenland, because

although the polar darkness often reigns (in Qaanaaq, the sun doesn't rise for three months!), it is never totally dark.

13. "The Board" is the local expression for the open meat and fish market found in all towns of Greenland. Here, you can buy the day's harvest — seal, whale, musk, reindeer, fish, and berries — straight from the fishermen, hunters, and pickers! The Board, whose Greenlandic name is Kalaaliaraq ("The Little Greenlander"), is usually located close to the port.

14. On January 6 ("Mitaartut" in Greenlandic), children dress in disguise, usually as rag witches who are only allowed to dance and make noises. When they knock on a door, they are invited inside.

15. The Greenlandic National Day is June 21 and is called Ullortuneq, meaning "The Longest Day," because of the summer solstice. It is celebrated with cultural activities, entertainment, and communal outdoor eating.

16. The Greenlandic flag, first introduced on June 21, 1985, is red and white, with a red semicircle symbolizing the midnight sun and a white surface the ice.

17. Greenland's geological history is the oldest in the world. Greenland is the site of the oldest rocks ever dated (3,700 million years). By way of comparison, the earth is reckoned to be 4,600 million years old.

18. Specialties of Greenland include reindeer meat (caribou), seal, whale meat, musk ox, fowl, shrimp, and fish.

19. There are only 55,000 inhabitants in all of Greenland.
20. Fishing accounts for 95.7 percent of all exports.
21. The northeastern part of Greenland is a protected national park. The size of France and England combined, it is the largest national park in the world.